VALIUM
DRAG

Linus,
You may have still had all your
hippy hair when this was set
but you'll hopefully recognize
the character that's based on
you.

Alfi

Alfie Cooke

KATALI EDITIONS

Valium Drag

Alfie Cooke © 2023
First Published 2023

Published by Katali Editions,
Gravesend, 2023

Printed in Great Britain by Amazon

VALIUM DRAG

When the winds blow eddies of dust through the street and you are the dust and the hours that fell away fall into the shadows,

All the things you dreamt of are gone.

TOMBSTONE

1

So there was Lucky Luke, all seven-foot-nine of his wiry frame, extended beyond the physics of culpable reality by a mighty quiff that rose up off the world in shady blonde above cheekbones you could cut through shanking sheet metal with. He was standing outside the doors of Mason-Hall, Tombstone's purveyors of over-priced stationery and notorious fountain pens that pissed their ink all over your hands and there was also the basement café, posh-haunt for all the old folks who could still afford it on the diminishing returns of their pensions. Luke was carefully rolling a navy, a bundle of blueys flapping in the Tombstone breeze from the top pocket of the drapest drape you'd see this side of Mecca, the Locarno, or any other dance hall-cum-bingo venue, from the Isle of Blight to the Finland station.

Of course, we'd all be wary of Lucky Luke as he was from a world that none of us recognised as being of our own and despite him being the rockingest rockabilly you'd ever get to know, he was also the most unpredictabilly of them all, friend and foe by turns and turn again to the wind, to taking the strain of the strut of his cut. Even Sophocles would be on his tip-toes when dancing through the scattereens of the Luckster's personality. But such is the charm of Tombstone-On-Thames.

Without a ware in the curdle, the strewth of lime resides in the chimes of the times of those choosing who not to die in the midlife of crisis and deciding to blow up and blow-out in the residue of panic: we do not live to leave in the wake of wasted mourning; to bantam burn for as legged-long as the days will dishonest allow; to not lay down like the fatted lamb for slaughter. We rise in kludged romance of revulsion, the revolutions of our strangled births plain for all to see in the residual chaos of broken-toed sandals as everything could be imaged for the imagination's machinations; we rise like lions shot with buck, like unleavened bread or the dead of tomorrow today, our bites no grace of lilac tights and the sham of sh'bang stoning our grossest considerations. We flap like the lap of the devil dogs, strained in our witness, forgone in the plaintive chant of shall and sharn't, the wicked wiles of the old dregs and their missive piles, the ploughed crowd crapulent of our vigors and vague manifestations. So been the woe-been, the ill-begot, the cruel. Show me the vanquished, the man-crushed, the tool. Expect the spunkman, the junkman, the cool.

We are now your face. We have stolen up your eyes & tho you cannot see we can see in the skull of your mind.

We are now the mind behind your eyes. We have stolen up your mattress grey & tho you cannot think we can shatter the synapse of your soul.

Shut out your concept; drop the bowl to break up the stone floor; reject everything; hold nothing; empty your wallet & pass your house-keys to the last stripper on the left that you meet. Only naked, truly naked, can you enter through the gates of hell.

Dante had a guide, but you get nothing. You deserve much less. I should give you just Chinese burns & a stick in the eye. But you are already blind. Blind in the heart. Blind in the mind of yuh kind.

So why have you come to this? Why is your desperate despot?

As a start we must start at the be- of belonging, the be-longing, the longing to be, to be someone of something, known to the knowable world beyond your own four walls of the cell of your criminal existence. In a crisis-time of desperate mis-identity, of lucked-out conformity to the uniformity of formulaic education – to be I and not they; to be us and not them. To be something more than the it of the id. Fircle found the faith within the throwbacks to earlier times that was the revival of a modernist movement, twenty years out of line with time. Beginning as a pre-pubescent skinhead with his discovery of ska'd blue beats, the rocksteady roll of the boots and braces celebrating the joy of Jamaica and the poor-white-trash of England's dreaming pyres, he stood himself out. But without the elements of coded kinship, with only the vermin scrag of bonehead bigotry around, he soon found himself drifting beyond, through suede-head, rude boy, tonic-toned suits and into the larger, more familial collection of Tombstone's own mod population. Most of those he knew were mods - Septic Longfellow, Smallbrick Ambulance, Chinese Dan. Even those who weren't would dress the same in a show of collective hysteria, these threads being the only clothing available in Tombstone market that didn't make you look like your dad on a bad day off. They listened to shared mixtapes of sixties beat bands, Detroit soul and wellered explorations of guitar and organ with just a little 2-tone rolled in for taste.

On a Saturday, they would gather in clumps around the market record stall, looking for the long-lost soul seven incher, never to be found; or outside the doors of OK Records; down at the riverfront arcade and hovering the magazine racks of Mason-Hall, hunting for jammy smears between the pages of the NME. If they had money in the pocket, they hung out at Papa's, crowding in at the back and taking over, with a circled round of refilled teas to keep them from being cast out to the four winds of Queen Street. It was a good place to hang for those just starting out on the long road to Brighton. The older faces who were working or claiming would arrive wearing threads from the Carnaby Caverns up in the city, their scooters sitting in the road outside and their parkas decked in scooter-run patches. And with them came their stunning girlfriends, black minis and ski-pants, Lonsdale handbags, Mary Quant and occasional skinheadgirl hair and shoes so patent you could see your face in them. Such was the source of all inspiration, the dream that one and all aspired to – the pristine-chromed vintage lammy with the beautiful girlfriend riding pillion, cruising to clubs they could then only dream of seeing inside. For them, there was only ever the Friday Nights at The Fleapit, with the floor-fillers of *Joe 90* and someone else's generation, greening the onions in the land of a thousand, beer-free and bundled at the end to the slamming doors of the tube station at midnight, a wild frenzy of dog-piled limbs and lamentation from which the girls all hid.

There was also the fact that Stax, the coolest scooter-boy anyone knew, with the coolest nickname under the sun would drop in to Papa's from time to time. Even the faces treated him as the diamond he was. He was built like the proverbial and could command the eyes just by the way he would swagger. Black flight jacket, green combats, the boxer boots – it was a look that so many, Fircle included, would soon seek to imitate after first seeing him. Some like Griffy Petrograd went for the jam-shoe smarts. The rest of them swore by the swagger of Stax.

While his local was technically The Formby, he only
ever went in there when all were on a crawl. Their usual
haunt was The Wolf's Head with its huge L-shaped bar
where they set their stall at the far north end and Guido,
the landlord, always willing to turn his one blind eye to
Fircle's underage drinking, so long as he did it in the
company of the Beerdozer and his grid. Before he'd
even left school, he was drinking down there so often
that Guido took him on as a regular. If he was serving
and he saw Fircle come in, he would flip the tap and start
a pint of black flowing. He'd started drinking there at
the age of thirteen, hanging out with his older kith and
kin, and over the course of several years established
himself as a known quantity, familiar to the staff,
recognised by regulars and known for trying in vain to
keep up with the heavy guzzlers like he Dozer – while
they would still be standing, he would collapse in a heap
outside, but so long as he didn't throw up in the bar or
attract the plod, Guido tolerated him. Then there was the
time that Fircle and Sophocles were sat at the bar,
fetching down rum with a dash of blackcurrant. Guido
noticed and proceeded to dance them through the range
of strange liqueurs that worked so well with the flow of
Jamaica. It was a wonder how God had never
introduced them to such tastes of joy any sooner.
Between the three, they worked through a bottle and a
half of the captain and seriously dented the
establishment's cocktail supply, much to the misery of
Guido's wife Renata, keeper of the accounts and orderer

of the ales. Worse was still to come for her, as Guido chalked the whole night's bill up to himself, a treat, he said, for what he called his valued customers. When they left at the end of the evening, Fircle and Sophocles could hardly stand. In the end, he made himself at home so much that for four years running he celebrated his eighteenth birthday there, drinking through to the early hours of a lock-in until they finally carted him out the door, leaving him to stagger, loose-limbed and lanky, back to his forsaken bed.

As a mod you were part of a clan, an extended family where you greeted others as brothers and sisters, standing together while those before you fled your fate or fury. At least that was the idea with being part of something. You stood side-by-side, shoulder-to-shoulder, like comrades at the barricades. In practice, this just involved mobbing together wherever you went and taking over by weight of numbers, much the same as they did in Papa's, a block of parkas and green trench coats swarming into a previously safe space to make it safer still for their own and fiscally mod-dependent.

Such was the scene when Smallbrick rolled into Papa's to tell them that he and Craps had been forced to flee out the back of Gypsy Dave's Arcade. What they were in there for was never as clear as a bucket of sick, as the safe arcade for mods was down by the river and they never went anywhere near Davy's, certainly not parka'd up to the eyeballs, or trench-coated as Ambulance was. It wasn't just asking for trouble. It was demanding it while pinning down Davy's granny with a giant, flaming dildo and screaming obscene filth in her geriatric ear. Still, as with the musketeers, an offence against one was an offence against all and the gauntlet had clearly been thrown to the floor. It would be a disgrace not to enter into the spirit of things and pick it up.

Instead of taking the direct route and cutting through the market, they hooked up their dog-tooth trousers and stomped off in the opposite direction towards The

Queen, rounded round her corner curves towards The King and only then took a right on to the High Street, collecting bodies as they went, til around thirty of them were then stalking down the hill. Fircle felt like he was in a cut scene from Quadrophenia and this was his Brighton Beach. It was all they could do to keep from chanting "we are the mods" at the bewildered Saturday shoppers as they went by. Nearly three dozen mods were closing in on the army surplus where they bought their parkas, gas capes and trench coats, itself almost opposite Davy's, when people started to exit the arcade. Just two at first and he knew it would be a slaughter. If they didn't run, then the shit would truly be beaten. Then more came out in twos and fours, the big bastards lining up across the front, sleeves rolled in readiness. They slowed their strut, and those towards the back began to wonder and worry. By fifteen yards, there were fifty or more and you had to wonder how Davy's could fit so many through its doors and as the mods slowed further to a standstill, at ten yards their numbers were overwhelming. Some had stopped altogether further back, tying their shoelaces they said, but judging what they knew of the safe ratios between running speed and distance. Even the few of their own big bastards had stopped, knowing already that the game was up, the deal was done and the outcome was already carved out in stone bar the bruising.

Like well-trained centurions in orderly retreat from the barbarian hordes, they all took a step back and prepared to take the second. And Davey's crowd, like the Natal Train, stomped down a foot forwards and its sound ricocheted off the high walls at either side. What followed was less of a battle and more of a rout as the mods were chased back the length of the High Street, small scuffles breaking out as the slower sods got caught and beaten, when not even the shopkeepers would magically appear to save them. So, nothing like the riots in Brighton of twenty years before and nothing they could praise themselves over. There'd been more in Davy's than anyone expected and a lot of the youngsters had shit a brick, leaving behind the weak and the brave and the lame to the fate of the fist. As they hit the crossroads, both sides in the skirmish began to disperse, Davy's lot sauntering off to find something better to do with their time than beat up mods, regardless of how much joy it gave and those in mostly parka'd packs of three or four, to find somewhere to nurse some wounds or restore some damaged pride. Some headed back to Papa's, some to the shelter of OK Records, while Fircle and his crew of two went and hid in the basement cafe of Mason-Hall, mainly because Drammy had an aunt who worked there, they were all skint and he could get the three of them a free cup of tea.

And there was also the problem of Lucky Luke's compatriot to contend with. While Sophocles' rockabilly mate was himself a formidable and potentially dangerous character to be side-stepped at all cost, 'Thunders', so called because of the word emblazoned in studs across the shoulders of his denim jacket, was known as a user of two big fists and heavy, toe-tec dealers that he wasn't afraid of wielding. Luke didn't often join the fray when Thunders went about his business but he did enjoy the spectacle. As he lit the smoke that he'd been rolling and blew a dark grey cloud into the air, he chuckled: he had seen Thunders rising up from his lean against the shop-front window and also the three parkas that had come out through the doors to his right and he knew what was coming up next.

They moved across to the other side of the centre, three young lads in their prized fishtails, trying to strut as if they ruled the world but still looking like the snot-nosed school kids they were, impressing none but themselves, swaggering all cocksure and busfared up to the nines when not half-an-hour before, they'd been running for dear life the length of the High Street. They were just the sort of pricks that Thunders liked to wallop.

The three mods sauntered outside Millets, looking at the monkey boots, when one of them felt the heavy hand of the world's injustice on his shoulder. The other two saw the sign and bolted before they too found themselves being punched to the floor. Unfortunately for Fircle, as the tallest by half-a-yard, he stood out from them as if wearing a neon-glowing hat saying "punch me". Thunders was more than happy to oblige him with that,

Fircle slammed down on to his back and as the fists of fury fell he tried to curl on to his side and into the fetal position. As the punches stopped he tried to get his hands up to cover his head, but Thunders had caught hold of the front of his parka and began slamming him down on to the concrete. To add some spice, as his victim's head bounced back off the floor, he slammed it back down again with a steel toe. It was a blinding game of football in which Thunders scored every goal.

At some point, Lucky Luke intervened. He'd met Fircle at some point before through Sophocles as both he and Fircle's brother would frequent the same clubs, often sitting together in the same all-night cafe in Rockville until the morning train rolled by, and while he may have been enjoying the entertainment, watching Thunders do his thing, he felt that he should maybe step in, just for the sake of friendship if nothing else. And then there was that b-side of that Piranhas hit, said getting beaten up was part of growing up, so it all fit into place, when you thought about it.

Fircle scraped what was left of himself off the floor and stumbled out to the bus stop, head spinning and teeth ringing. The other two were still there calmly waiting. No one said anything about what had just happened. All for one and one for all.

Lazaroon soon found that the world was a place of science, the course of the cause of the cawing affect an' the ration o' the reason for treason. For the laz it was the maz of the mooz that slung from the blues of the booz and in leaving the house, there had to be the clause for the many effect that he needeth. It would always be his way to struggle with the juggle – he drank to be blind to his own petty horrors but if there was a good enough reason to hold court, it slowed his consumption enough to keep him from a keel in the korner. Cause and effect. He went out, so he was bombed on heavy, but, if talking, it was more a strategic hit than carpet bombing. Their first forays were shambolic, symptomatic of the betrayal of their singular-sexed education. It was a hard enough task thinking about how to talk to girls when they had barely seen one for three years but what was worse as a curse was that so few of them actually knew of any or in which of the seven hells to find them. To begin, their parties were like a meeting of the masons, some secret, sacred cult of the masculine immatures. They would stand around with their cans of warm beer talking lamely to the same people they sat next to in class, all of them wondering how to break the sad cycle. In the end, it fell to Galliard Crane to save them from their onanism.

Galliard was friends with Tulsa from the old days before education swung a meat cleaver betwixt woman and the beast and Tulsa was not just of their age but knew oh so many others of her kindred kind. Galliard, it seems, not only already knew them all but he also had the gift of gabble and charm. Something none of the rest possessed in any great stealth. It was a skill that Fircle badly needed to possess as he'd already found that if there was something to do with his mouth other than guzzle then he could hold back the dual tides of vomit and passing out and stand himself in better stead with learning how to communicate with those they had begun to quaint acquaintance themselves with.

But the signs and the signals were there from the early mourning: the loss of control, the loss of any ability to refrain once off the leash and the growing need to have a crutch to lean and bevel that would let him feel at one with the universal, if only for the time it took to find himself back in the shock of sobriety.

Fircle Lazaroon had never been himself a belonging of anyone or anywhere person. He had drifted through the pauses of existence as a rogue rat drifts through each sermon of the sewers, holding on to no home for long before the family moved on elsewhere and he had to start again. He could hold on to a fingertip grip for only so long before the wife of the world would once again hammer at his bones to force his fall. Such were those means of existence that he built himself a cage to lock away all the sense that the world would never make and set it with a match upon its kindling.

Tombstone had its own circuit of drinking dens that would be stalked by the various and sundry. Just as in every town, those on the fringes of estates would always be fed by the local beast, and you haunted their doors only as the guest of a known quantity. Like the Chuzzlebutt that sat on the edge of its namesake, or the Rhinoceros' Horn that lay out to the west. Such pubs are effectively local-led community centres, somewhere for those that lived near or by to go to relax amongst their own, away from customers, managers, bosses and outsiders. But with few exceptions, those sitting in the centre of town were open territory, changing hands between deadbeats and soulboys, moochers and trojans without too much of a usual quarrel and mostly with the ebb and flow of each new year's fresh faces.

So while the Three Crows was then mostly a hangout for the deadbeats, and the Wardour was the adopted home of the mods, the Jetty held an open door, so all could take a turn getting messed up on their Dingoe's Butt ale, always sold by the half, smooth to down and capable of removing any and all control you had over your legs by the second dram, leaving you to jibber on the floor in a wreck.

Up the hill to the south, the King's Arse was a shared reference while the Duke of Cheddar was haunted by soulboys and their queens and, further on, the Tramway was again a home for deadbeats and moochers. Both the Shades were taken by trojans, with outsiders like Sophocles being allowed in The Lamp only by virtue of his connections, and never in the company of Lowen who had way too much hair for his own good. Then there was the Cadiz which took all comers, so long as you could squeeze along its corridor-like standing area between the wall and the bar that ran from the front through to the back on Stoner's Street. The real oddity was The Irish which always seemed to be busy, was slap bang dead centre of Tombstone but was used by none of the young turks. No one ever gave a reason why and no one ever went in to find out.

Fircle and his brother tended to move between The Tram and The Crows, stopping on occasion in the Frog & Lemon, it being the new-scented invent of the wine-bar, which women seemed to like to do a lot of standing around chatting in, possibly attempting to bring some civility to their otherwise barbaric Saturday evenings. Boyfriends would stand in quiet desolation as they listened to talk of soft furnishings and marriage favours while panpiped pop filtered down on them from hidden speakers, often with the unfamiliar shape of a wine glass in their hands, dumbfounded as to what to make of this strange and grown-up world in which they now found themselves. Men had been seen to enter their doors on a first date only to emerge two hours later with a wedding booked, three kids on the way and a thousand yard stare of blank, abject horror.

Few who were yet to troth the ploth of the pledge ever lasted long in the mouth of the Frog. For Sophocles, trams and crows made more equilibric sense, both being within staggering distance of the last bus, which admittedly they rarely made, and sooner rather than later, they gave way to the pull and took the road one way or t'other. So the sophocletic oath, his hipster Wallace close by his side, Fircle somewhere behind and the sometime appearance of Wallace's buckle, Desirae, who Fircle had dated once in an atrocity best left to the abyss, would stride the street that lead them to the blasting arms of the Tram's open and loving embrace.

By that state of the evening there was never a chance to sit on a Saturday night, although women always seemed able to squeeze another of their own on to the benches. The men all clung like Berbers to the Rif mountain precipice of the bar, ready in their minds to call for a final pint when the bell was wrought and rung. As it took its toll, the brothers threw together the last of their shrapnel - bus fare included - to muster up enough for a final brew, often a shared, single pint, before facing the long and sobering walk home.

So, Bodene's was the initial option, being as they were always slow through from the back. Working in tandem one could hoist a bottle into the inside pocket while the other took up a blocking position at the till. With luck, it would be the old man, half-blind and feeble of foot, and while they waited for him to pigeon-step out you could reach across to where the smokes were stacked on the left-hand shelves. Camels and navy were up towards the back wall, out of arm's harm's way but the silks were easy pickings and, from what he'd seen, the flavour of choice when rolling the resin. It was also the cigarette of choice for most of the girls they knew, so having a pack handy always made good sense. Loon nabbed himself twenty and waited for the old boy to make it through the door so he could get some salty old sea-dog for rolling later. As they walked out, Crane clanked in time with each step, with four cheap reds weighing down his coat tails.

Eventually, they burned Bodene's too often, with the old boy's wife then always out front and on guard. They would still get what they needed for a night out but it meant paying and as the prices were always better elsewhere, their alternative became the Amen Corner, so called because Amen, you could get what you wanted, no questions. The best deals were always on the sweet cider, and as that was also the preference for most of those same girls, it made good sense to do the extra walk down to Soulville and stack up on stocks before venturing forth.

Lowen Behold had the habit of twisting the catweazle of his beard as he spoke of the many great wonders of the leadbellies of the universal song, excitedly rambling, all the more so when the mystic was aflame, at which point it became a ponderous tic in time with the rock back and fro as his eyes set off for the distance. He had made himself the mad maven of fine americana, of the blues of hill-folk and the hills of blues-folk, and when Fircle first uncovered the sounds of Uncle Bob's nasal plaintive, Lowen was on hand to point him in the direction of Woody, Huddie and the blinded lemon and the oh so many houses of the rising sun, the oh so many resolutions for the coming revolution in his mind. The world opened up its wonderment, sounds to be found in the rarely rummaged racks of Tombstone library and nowhere but nevermore else. Lowen had raised and raided all there was, committing to tape the vinyl lake that flowed with ebb and tides of time and twelve-bar refrains, plaintive souls singing over strings of six and nine an wailing mornings an lonesome nights, their wheeling reels reprised of jigs and peals, the pearls of simple songs of complex wisdom, of love and the slipknot, death and the rails and the dust.

Unknown to the beknownst of the fak of Fircle, his reputation was already going on before him in the manner of a runaway train. The compadres fully expected to find him raiding the medicine cabinet for answers wherever he went and the girls, while fully expecting him to attend in all his darkness, assumed the worst, expected the raid, and asked of others that they check that his pockets were clean before entry.

"Welcome to my madness," he would gleam with an intox sparkle, as he took to his throne, a pipe of drum pre-stoked at his lips and an ethanol twink in the corner of his eye. The comrades looked to adore his flagrant blatance while the girls all shook from his balkan fragrance and his schemes. Their tolerance taught to the tensions of split, the wary would edge themselves to the salvation of coherence, the boys of bankers-draught sons who could always show the fair degrees of restraint, something of which Fircle and his coterie of wild hunting dogs seemed incapable.

They would drink til they fell or fall in tattered tears, the ramrod of oblivion's eyes eagerly searching for the lex luthered liver. They would roar with fierce abandon at the stars and stomp to the go-go beat demanding more and more and always more beyond. Galliard, Bullett, Lazoon at the front and centre, Hobart Cripps in the chaos of his own mad spiral down surrounded by the landfill site of empty cans. These five hundred fellows had moved themselves tangential to the lure of The Fiend and had welded themselves in marriage to whatever came beyond, wherever it could be found. If they hadn't anything in the pocket, they would go on a house hunt, swallow what they found and wash it all around until something started to happen. Septic Longfellow could always be relied upon to amp up the process with the phetamine's rush for those that wanted to blister their heels and mothers had others who could bring in the mystic and the coloured skies. But these few had found there was something both enigmatic, charming and alarming about their own leap into the unknown: the forage of the feast, the classes A thru to Zed and the shock of the newt.

They were young and they knew there was no hope for a future. If they danced themselves to death on the disco'd floor, they knew it was a glorious end to be had. If they charged headlong into the bottle and broke the glass of their mind on its empty shell, they knew it was naught but the bitter crush of the world's jealousy of their misspending. If they laundered the midnight's decay and scribed the line beyond the broken will of the wheel, they knew that sanity was but the last repose of those too afraid to live. Such was all a victory in a war that would claim the many of them as casualties but just so long as they could keep from surrender for long enough to proclaim aloud for 'liberty or death'.

Like them all, Fircle was neither leader nor follower, just one more lost soul in search of the hole inside that could never be filled. Somehow they had found themselves as lambs to the self-same slaughterhouse, so bonded they together in bleat, accepting the archeology of their existence as the great wolf that needed so bad to be brought to the heel of hell. And they turned the angst of the anx on the hole of the soul and sought to find a fire they could burn the world with, if they didn't burn their fingers first.

Upon leaving the Institute of Grammatical Surrection, each escapologist would be donated a gift of thanks from the communities that had long suffered the ghosts of their intransigences. For some, the buggery was obtusely delivered, like a quaking sermon, which others felt as the full squelch of lube upon their souls. When it came to Lazaroon, he was hauled back from the cartage crate he had locked himself into and lead to the basement of their hatred. Having connived his own tunnel out, he had been billed for a stint with the iron maiden but thankfully Sweaty Mormon was in there, refusing to leave, and Fisty Gristo was dancing the Colonel Tom hot plate. So despite being long of the leg already, Fircle was tied to the rack by ankle, armpit and ear, to be stretched beyond the ken of his sinews. Consequently, he left their loving embrace a full seven foot in his socks with his lobes at such right angles that forevermore he would wear weighted diving boots to avoid blowing away in the wind. His gait now gangly and ducking, sloping through doorways as his knees struggled to gauge the directions his feet could take, while they had failed to fully learn him, to the ghosts of their goat, they nevertheless had taught him the leanest lesson, however inconsistent of value and undeserving of a merit badge he found it.

There wasn't one before and there wouldn't be another one to follow its footsteps, whether in spotless spats or kitten heels. The only ever Tombstone-on-Thames Jazz Festival, riding on the back of the boom of bopping that had swelled from the unknown straits of bygone eras and half-forgotten heroes to become the big new thing on the washed-up shores with demon swingers like Courtney and the Warriors, the scene-on-the-green with the lonely shepherd, and the blakey'd beat of Tommy chasing down the tenor solos and crashing like a giant wave. A new music for a change in time.

The festival itself was a handful of acts packed into a marquee in the back garden of The Miller's Chuff, one of the pubs lurking on the fringes of the centre but which was an open house to one and all due to its ye olde village appeal. It was all low-key, in the way that all such chance enterprises are, hoping just to cover the costs at best and maybe even claw something back to build upon, maybe a foothold for Limbo Debs to build a career as either a funk-fired pianist or an impresario.

Fircle'd been in there a few times before, celebrating people's birthdays after the rumours around what had been done to Ratso Cummerbund's house turned out to be true and no one was willing for quite a while to have their homes similarly trashed. He would go to chew the fat with the others from his own corner of hell and to catch up with Galliard who always seemed able to charm his way into any event, but mostly he went on the slim chance that Eclipse Romain would be there. On their first meeting, Fircle had been hit with the smit, steamrolled down by the way and the wherefore she looked and looked at him. She never was in the Miller's as it seemed she by then frequented the Admiral Shanks, which as well as having a dancefloor of sorts, also had a lot of older guys who would have crushed him into dust.

In all those times, he'd never made it out to the Miller's back garden and assumed as everyone else did, that there wasn't one. But there they were, under a ropey blue tarpaulin, listening to various little combos, one of the best of which had been Django Sprotborough, an old boy who looked like someone's granddad's granddad but who did a nifty-fingered turn on some gypsy-jazz standards, just himself, his guitar and a cranky amplifier perched precarious on a bar stool.

As the atmosphere was drift and summer, Lowen pulled out his stash and did the deed while Sophocles went for another round of black. Up til then, Fircle had been fine with the fiend as his best escape but when Lowen passed it along the line, he felt that he couldn't say no: they were drinking, it was summer and Charlie Parker was being played between sets: what more reason did a young man need? He drew in deeply as he'd seen the others do and felt the world just disappear away from under his feet as he floated away to the opening bars of *Anthropology*, spellbound. This was the magic that was missing in his mind, the dreams of mystic-eyed wonder, the wisdom, the soporific stun of the wild fantastic.

Sophocles had gone along to support his friend, Limbo Debs, whose band was the seasoning before the greens of Tommy Chase's headlining quartet. Debs' piano kicked in over a deft blue note groove and all the heads began to bob. Some danced and others beat along on the tables in drum-frenzy fantacism. And, oh my, was this not the good gravy of sound: pints of black, a taste for the Lowen's mystic and the racing rhythms of the lion and the wolff belting out. And then it stopped. Dead. In its tracks. Limbo had seemingly lost it. Not his playing, which was still fine, but the next number had changed the format. The trio were joined, in an attempt to create a sellable seat to fit the pop-jazz boom, by two female singers with weak voices and seldom swing. They were living the jazz life in a search for chop suey. For the rest of their set, the band alternated between instrumentals and vocals, between sublime and indifferent, or more accurately, between the damned good and the bloody awful.

At the end, they all knew, Sophocles, Lowen, Fircle and Upnor, that something needed to be said and the Soph was duly elected by the slide of a land to sacrifice himself and break the news that the slots for what turned out to be Limbo's girlfriend and her partner in crime weren't just bad but were off the scale. He'd been gone about ten minutes, the whole while that Tommy was setting up his kit, before he returned.

"I couldn't do it," he dejected, "I just couldn't do it. Everyone kept coming up and saying how great it was and he looked so pleased and proud of himself. I couldn't break his heart like that. And besides, that's his girlfriend - she was stood there clinging to 'is arm the whole time. What you meant to say in that situation?"

They all laughed but a drum rolled up from the bowels of the burning earth, rising up through the magma'd ranks before bursting open the cracking of the crust and splitting the world asunder. This was the dime of time-keeping. This was the big beat burn of the Tommy Chase Quartet as they stormed the Tunisian night.

For the long and the rust of all that is complicit in the dawn, guilty of the day and troubled by betrayal of the night, comes the creeping at yuh windows like the silence of widowed tongues detached from their epilogual glot. No to the whisper of the go and the gone, the bloody rip, the scream of gunshots bounding the street-lit; no to the fiesta of gut and groove, of flailing wail and all yuh lost tomorrow.

Always such an argument to bear, and always such a need to be knowing of the outcome. Way back to the when of beginning and the glass shattered first on the floor from the staggered stars and the ransacked sacking of the sky. And the hidden-from-the-light locks down in its cellar, the beast within hid from the terrors of help and no. A sickness. A shard. A dance with a devil, kaleidescoping the jungle of days, with histories burnt like bridgeless rivers of desire. Gropes make rake at the rollock of rites and ritual and the touch of the bottle, its tongue to tickle the tonsils, its sweet kiss loving like none of another, the charm of the arm and the saints of the taints be the arse of all that after arises. Lush is the lover, the longer, the languid brush with death. Lush is the sweeped caress, the hand run through the hair and the holding to the bitter's eve has left but just a shadow, nothing more. Lush is the calling card of the concubine, the Buddha's breath, the word of God and the way.

Be it the bride or fillet the wide, the hope of the hill on which all enemies falter or fail in remissive conflict. The revolution steps its game in its might and mighty is the possible of nothing. All men be weak to your hand. All women be loves to began, motorbike tremors of their emotional content. Stab at the barrel's store-house, drain the dram til its ethanol fog departs. Nothing can be left unaccounted. No one lets you leave unless you harness all fear of all things with a screw-top cap. Such is the way to hide from the world - the bottle. Such is the way to deal with desire - the bottle. Such is the way to find faith in God - the bottle. Once this hand lays soft upon your brow, then none would be heard to call you back to task or to time. Only the kiss of the bottle does this. Only the langored, long, hot summer of lush. Only, again, the bottle to have and to hold.

Fircle and Galliard clanked their way down to the park, full of the summer of a dreamer's weekend. They were on their way to meet up with the Twins Romain and oh for the jig of joy of being in love.

The gill Galliard was, of course, known by then to be albatrossed in the arms of Shillelagh Romain, but for the dirk of the firk there was still some ways to tread before he could ever be in a position to have reached the same hallowed halls of a jane austen novella-salad with her sibling. The catamaran that would be a touch of grace in the wilderness was oh so defiant, belligerent, indeed, to be gained or said with the much adored Eclipse, being herself the gift of the grail to be sought by one an all and so having herself a regular cadre of lotharic beaus to cling on in jest. And oh with a wondrous wave of her hand she would scatter them like crows, all a-cawing one another to the blame. It was such a sight to be seen and so was she. But smit as he was, Fircle lacked the socials to not be a full pair of spectacles of himself, being without the smooth cajool of one like Galliard or a sup of the lush at his side.

He was launching such a sup when the johnny panic came down from on high in the not-so hushed tones of Crane:

"Hide the bottle! Hide the bottle!" gushed the gill, side-stepping to switch his coat across the cider that his accomplice had been necking.

Fircle feeble fumbled it under his jacket, wiping his mouth with the back of his hand:

"Whazafug?"

"Car at twelve o'clock. Their dad's driving. Trust me. You do NOT want him seeing you swigging. Eclipse has told him we're both good presbyterian cloisters to be trusted like jehosophat's witness."

Galliard swung back to face the open window on the driver's side with a smile and Fircle looked sheepy at the floor.

"Good day to you, Mr Romain, sir," he helloo'd like a choirboy, fully intent on acting the innocence of his fictional youth. Mr Romain just sternly nodded as if issuing a violent threat or a sentence of death. All he said was "Four o'clock" and this to his daughters, never once taking his eyes off of Galliard, who struggled not to buckle under the onslaught. Even as he disappeared into the driven distance, this cogent image of purity and honour could feel the father's eye burning an arc-weld into his skull via the rear-view mirror.

"Jinkers," he finally breathed in light relief, "and shall we adjourn to a quiet corner?" and he took Shillelagh's hand and lead the way. Eclipse looped her arm into the hoop of Fircle's.

"Come on," she said, "pass me the cider you're hiding and tell me what the world must be told of love and poetic angst."

16

In the pitch of the bombing of Laudenum, a plane had strayed away from its curse'd course, missed the mustang base on the outer most skirts of Tombstone and bombed seven different shades of shit out of a field and a small clump of trees in part of an old country manor's estate. With the decline of the west and the rise of the fellaheen, the council had landscaped the bomb-craters from thirty years before into something less brutally honest, creating a country park for the proles. What it left after landscaping was a series of wide, shallow hollows, some barely visible without the aid of a spirit level, but one just sweet enough to make the greatest little picnic spot. Galliard seemed to know of it well but never told how or why. It was deep enough so that by laying flat in the middle, you couldn't be seen from any angle, and even when sitting on the sloping sides very little could be seen from beyond its limit.

Eclipse, in a vest top and shorts too short to bear, took charge of the music and their sleepy hollow soon filled with the falling, purple rain. Later they switched through some of Galliard's new wave and even took on board that tape of Diz that Fircle had left in the drawer. But while bop may well have met the big band, it was the princely ring that stuck clear and forever in his head. Galliard passed around the cider, from nowhere producing a couple of plastic cups that he passed with the bottle that he handed across to Shillelagh, leaving he and Fircle to neck theirs straight - less refined but, they figured, more in keeping with their cartoon characters.

So while the girls got tipsy and the boys got drunk, they talked of anything and everything: schools, music, love, boys, the world and all its ransomed heck.

17

"But you've got to let me have it back, okay. You've got to bring it round. Bring it round yourself."

Eclipse put the tape into his hand which she held in both of hers. His heart was thumping. The arteries in his neck throbbed as if pleading to burst, the cheeks on his face burnt hot then cold then hot then colder still in time with the pound pound pound and god this girl really was the most beautiful woman in town. Absolutely the most beautiful and yet here she was, talking to him, talking to HIM! Holding his hand. Nobody else. No one. Here. At this time. To him. Holding his hand in hers and smiling.   Since first he'd met her on Tulsa's introduction, himself half-drunk and her with a can of beer that she never seemed to sip from, he was lost in her wonderful smile, the soft flick of her short hair and oh-dear-lord those eyes, those eyes, those eyes but oh so much that smile of all smiles.

She leant her head forward and they kissed as the Inuit do, snuffling noses, foreheads together, innocently affectionate due to the inconvenient fact that her mother was watching like a hawk on the hunt from her car. He felt her eyelashes brush his cheek and she sighed and stepped back and then away, one hand still clinging to his til their fingers slipped.

Fircle then spent the next month listening to nothing else, playing her tape over and over until the rewind button wore down its clogs and rattled its spokes, but however much the purpled rain fell and the kids went crazy, from that Sunday in July he never saw her. She

45

was never at the parties where everyone met: not at Coney Winegum's, where he and Galliard set themselves up in a garden tent and held court like Bedouin tribesmen, regaling their visitors with tales of piracy and wisdom; not at the one where he took something from the medicine man, kicked his spleen and shattered the lush through his eyeballs and Coney had dragged him out of the rose bushes to calm the banshee that was wailing out of his soul; and then the final one at Tulsa's she'd missed, when Shillelagh came alone, split from the gil of the galli, and both Fircle and she had been too tipsed to turn away the other's advance. They had huddled together, long and lorn, beneath the open stairs but never spoke of it afterwards.

So the Eclipse wasn't seen for the final time, no fanfare fare-the-wells, no waving off the ship at the docks. As with all such one way loves, its loss isn't seen or heard but only felt in the impact marks of a body slamming down on the pavement from greater heights. Eclipse just seemed one day to disappear like mist in the morning sun. He heard her name as a whisper one time, when someone mentioned that she'd said he hadn't bothered knocking at her door to hand her the tape she'd leant but instead just let it drop through the letterbox. His heart ark-royaled to the depths when he heard these words. He could have stopped and knocked but it was morning, he was sober, and without the courage of the dutch inside, the terror of rejection stalked through his soul with a cleaver and he ran. She had pleaded with him to take it back himself, to not post it through the door but gripped by the flat cast of sanity's dead rival, he ran to hide away, forgetting the warmth of her kiss, the touch of her hand on his, the flick of her soft-washed hair and the scent of her skin. He ran like the jesus lizard skimming the surface of the lake does. He ran like Robert Johnson, fleeing for his life from the hellhound that would forever be on his tail, even after death. Except Fircle hadn't got anything for the selling of his soul: no guitar picking skills, no wealth and no love. Just a hellhound of his own design hunting him down for all time.

LAUDENUM

The iron face fell from the stars of the sky's most unloved cousin who strapped his spanish stone mason crap-hammer to the grave. Ye gods are dead-mongers of poverty, their elastic mouths split like charnel remains – til only the long-list-lovers regrow their bones. Jacky Oh fallen to the way of the wail, the sail, the sally forth and fallow, the shake of a feather is graceless and taut, the remarks of remarque are ringing in your ears. The sliver of a quiver down your spine spots you dead an your tracks disenfranchise the franks, the francescas, the frans flanned their funnels, tunnels tumultuous in their awning. Shorn of all ingodliness to spoke in the reverence of never. A door slams because it's been there been square, the daddios dominos erect and awaiting to dunk the flunk the fablioso, the critical mass of messinas, the dram of the dreamer. Drunkards spew lothario wishes across the dance floors of history at well-worn ladies and comfortable boots. The pleasure of a firework virus scams its scrawl up the clag of Klang, the sharp of shape-shifting, broken-nosed virgins stumbling in the wilderness that eats itself out of its desire. Love falls its naked brow upon the failing designs of autumn. The monastic onanism of the trees cries its bleat across the night, the dance of scattered hopes falls face down in yesterday's dirt, the coliseum of feinted women.

The Bank of the Dark Satanic Mills had a big building up in the Zoroastrian Temple district, just on the crippling edge of the city-in-the-city where your soul goes to die. Blank grey with dirty windows that wouldn't open and nothing on the outside to indicate there was anything of any worth within its walls. It didn't even bear the bank's name. The reason for that was that every cheque signed in or out passed through its doors, processed in deniable secret in an age before the digital era stripped everything bare-boned and slippy. Fircle spent two months there, short-shifting, cooking the books and claiming all the overtime that was offered him.

He was a porter and he'd been taken on because all the regulars said there was far too much work for them to get it all done within a normal day's labour, that being the reason they were all having to claim so much overtime. Yet no one who worked there did even a standard day, let alone all the extras they were claiming, so the bank took on a couple of temps to help take up the slack. It didn't work any. All that happened was that the temps would be sworn into an existing secrecy and signed off for the same hours as everybody else.

"You've got me hours wrong," Fircle had pointed out at the end of the first week when he took his timesheet back.

"No," said Organ Morgan firmly, "these are the hours you worked and if you say any different, we all get in the shit. Alright?" Organ looked at them both and they looked at each other and smiled.

"Fair enough."

"Secondly, if you're off sick - and don't be as it makes it 'ard for the rest of us to get away early - don't phone your office, you phone me. Your timesheets'll be done the same as this, so if you phone your office, they'll ask questions and we're all back in the shit again. Here, we don't want no questions from anyone. No one asks any questions and I don't give 'em no answers. How long you 'ere for?"

"As long as you want."

"Jus' til the end of the Summer."

"Okey-cokey. You, you'll go down in my book like the rest of us and get the same paid 'oliday. You - university is it? - I'll mark you down for a few days between now and whenever you go, so you both get a few days paid. Okay? I know it all sounds a bit crooked but... er... well, it is to be honest, but if you both play ball, we all go 'ome with more in our pockets? You both okay with that?"

"Fine with me," said Leon.

"Fine with me," said Fircle.

So that was it, working fewer than twenty-eight hours a week and being paid for forty, plus the weekly bonus they got for being trusted to carry around sealed boxes of cheques around a sealed room and then hoovering up the rubber bands that they all came wrapped in afterwards. The only hardship was that the windows wouldn't open, so by midday everyone was sweating like proverbials.

It was while working there that Fircle met Samantha, although saying he met her stretches the myth beyond the credibility of its capacity. She worked there, like a love-struck puppy, Fircle followed her round hoping for treats, making a point of ensuring that he was the one dropping off the boxes of cheques at her station, clearing up after her and generally making a right-royal pain in the arse of himself. And that was just about it. She was somewhere in her mid-thirties, maybe twice his age, dressed all in black with wide flowing skirts that sashayed as she moved and with her long blonde hair that came straight down her back to end at the tops of her thighs, he thought she was adorable. What she thought about him was probably less complimentary.

He would wish her good morning, but unlike many of the other women in the sort room, she would never acknowledge him by name, or even that she knew what it was. She might say 'thanks' in her polite, surrey-by-way-of-essex accent and that was just about it, until she called "box!" for someone to drop off the next load of cheques. Feeble attempts at small talk fell by the wayside and as the summer dragged on, he was left to dream his schoolboy dreams.

The walk to the wick, the tower, the terror, seventeen floors down to crack the slabs and a view out over Laudenum to see the growing glowing skies flooded smogged orange, out over the cathedrals, the scrapers, the scorpions, the city of the dreadful night. Off the six at the end of the line's line, past Jane Gray's Head, the shittered shuttered shops, the rank of wheeled drums sitting below twenty storeys of waste chutes above and the lift that seldom happened. Such was the home of Sophocles Lazoon and Franny Gaslight, the daughter of a general on the cold war front, who had travelled the bases of Europa in search of belonging and now found herself washed up on the shores in the far off reaches of Candlewick Creek.

It was there that Fircle ran to on a Saturday afternoon having hawked his way through record racks and bookstacks in search of hidden gems that no one knew or understood in their buckets. It was there that he ran to when the lush of his life wracked his body into three falls and a submission. And it was there that he ran to to hide from the horrors of his known existence and the lonely crypt he so often found he'd fallen into.

He could put on records and stare out over the ghosts of the city and long for the days of peace and tunguskan serenity while Sophocles would be cooking up a storm in the kitchen and Franny would roll out the naval mystic to mellow the fall of the night's bleak wishes. A bottle of red and an eighth, *Coltrane in Birdland* on the stereo and the Laudenum glow. And such are the things that all such dreams are made of.

There in the stands of glory do we echo our over-bites against the slouch hat of freedom, the beaten beatitudes of every beatrice living or to have lived. There in the terraces of turpentine do we serpentine the rivers of humanity, in a bare staggered hall, the orchestral chairs stacked out to form the arc of the covenant to come. The bright lights of summer and stage shedding the scene to blank, artificial restraints, cold to the touch and lame to the crutch; unforgiving of forgotten memory. The members of the jury began to settle themselves in awe, among them Jamal and Nuriddin, brothers from the days before the rap left the trap, the last of the poets still lost in the loose of the noose of amerika, a homage to the hero, to the man who made us possible, to the omelette altophonist, the chaos, the Coleman, whose band followed on from the orchestra, taking their time in the prime of their pews, all fully electrified, all fully phased to harmolodic synchronicity of all the universal minds.

The evening had been kicked into its existence by the powerhouse that was the big bang of the even stevens of Evan and the straight horn of hope, who entered to the empty and proceeded to thunder the drum-beat of life for a full-fisted forty-five, fortified minutes of rolled lightning, beating the sopranic Parker'd pads without but once a pause to breathe, as fools believe. And the beach is dread and the running sun burned and buried next the scores of the souls of the damned among us all and lo did the lord come down to revere and all was the cracking of Bolden walls and the shatter of Ayler'd glass to a piercing, multi-phonic scream. Then he bowed. Then he was gone. Gone in the air.

But after the rebuilding of redress and the repair and the dimming again of the lights, another roll of lightning crackle and the son of the Texan twister began his beguine, setting off the storm-built band of holy sound and intrigue steaming headlong into the unknown night ahead of crash-boom-bang and broiled by bass and the strings held over their heads vibtrato'd sound forms that pierced the room and punctured the lung and jagged the world into agreeing its terms of surrender. And as if from a secretive passage, Ornette flew to the centre of the stage, half-missed by many too lost in their delirium, too fragile to be buried beneath a swell of sound so heavy the stones of the earth came to crumble and cry. And thus began and begat his ode to the underside of a stolen land, the stolen people, the dust-filled Okie skies and the upperlachian high. As, oh, how the edges of history blurred into phosphorus and the magnesium burned like searing to the hilt like lye for the eye. Such be the bye of the skies of all Americas now, before and forever after, such be the Seminole Sioux of forgotten testimonies, crooked deals written out of the land and hidden beneath concretes of injustice, loud be the lay of the land to the joy of the toy in plaintive ode to the memories of Don, lost to the wheel of the rack and the rain, of painful memories of every repression thrown down in the crucible of hatred, all painted out with the colours of sound displacing the weight of all our human failings.

When you head to the north end of Laudenum, you find it holds a series of weirdly territorial boundaries, none of which make meagre sense in either spatial or temporal classifications, relying on purely cultural fluctuations as their defining grace: there'd be the 'Jewish Quarter', the 'Muslim Quarter', the 'new town', the 'posh bit', the 'trendy posh bit', the 'poor bit', the 'grim bit' and so on, into an infinite number of little chunks that no one on the outside understood or could ever hope to command a knowledge of.

For himself, once he got as far as the lock at the far north end of The Clampdown, Fircle was pretty much lost and unless he had someone acting as guide and interpreter, he rarely ventured beyond the edge of the known world in case such a trek to the source of denial resulted in the lost temptations of Mayan progress and he'd never to be heard of again.

You could tell there was something out there, just as the stars tell you that other galaxies exist out there in the universe, but just because a bus had 'Boundary Green' written on its front, it didn't mean he was going to go out and explore just what that boundary held in store. For all he knew, the bounds of that green weren't the city limits but the very edge of the earth itself, beyond which was only the bleak abyss of all our nightmares and not even Charles Napier was brave enough to ever step out that far.

23

Blurred slurs blurt the incoherent rant, the rambled, ramshackle shock o' the old familiar ranks seeded, rooted, run riot in the brain, the brawn run to mouth run-off with the riotous wife of reason of once more one too many. Churning chatters rattled through rotted teeth sick-stained in decay so the telling gets told of old repetition repetition repetition of welsh'd head awash by it all a thousand times before and laying lies levels, the bragadaccio'd bull shit butt shack crack of no, not that, that's not what I said that's not what no, no, you, no, juss listen listen to domineer-defeat, to browbeat to break and on and on without escape, without respite without a rest, without a gasp of air into the breast to single solemn-handed beat retreats from every spirited soul in a sobered room, those left embattled by boorish proclamations checking wit and wisdom at the door, at the screw-top lid, at the ring-pull's restraint, delayed in stumbled thought of always one more tale to tell to top another's, always knowing another unfunny yarn about just that very thing that no one ever laughs at and nothing whatsoever to be done with it other than tolerate the torrent, be fed the ceaseless stream, the endless team of jabbered nonsensical slap across the face of reason or reasonable behaviour, like even does anyone ever put up with the guttural garbage, the word after word after word after word of utter, utter shite and gobshite.

Up there in The Clampdown, the condemned, camdemned mile of road from the tube to the dock of the lock where everything of any use or ornament of aspiration to the world beyond the boundaries around the spectres of feudal restraint could be found. Streams of vinyl running through the basements, markets full of the used and well-worn and then there was the compended store at the bridge where every book they'd ever warn you about could be found, from childish revelations of barriered blocks to the marquis' many days and the love of old bull's spare ass. The Clampdown was a mine of rare and honoured gems, there to be rifled and roared over, weighty vinyl in unplayed vintage, ragged railroad strides, implausible instruments repaired beyond recognition to make otherwise unplayable sounds of fickle sonances to call the angels home again.

Fircle would roll himself northern from Ray's in the centre of the city to spend his Saturdays spending, finding himself the po' boy slouch of a hat to match the scattered poesy of his hero. Damn was it ever a fine place to spend the last days of all non-existence of nothing and beingness.

Further up the line was a corner on the edge of The Fortress that held the strange beauty of the Pro Brass Music Emporium. Built into the triangular fork between the thoughts of the fort and the white cliffs of Ardiles Farm Estate, it was brimming to skimming with every manner of brass and woodwind seen by the mind of man or the will of woman: a great bare baritone, laquerless, the grey metal calling for a mulligan stew, the golden tenor demanding *Alabama* and the bright bell of a Liston slide. And then, just about the only thing he could hope to afford in all his dreams, a silver-plate cornet styled like the one played by the King, all ripe and ready for the chiming blues along Rampart Street. Ninety sobs. He had sixty and, lo, was there nothing to be done but for Sophocles to stump up for the rest and Fircle would owe him forever and he left with the coolest cased cornet at his side. All he needed now was Joe Oliver's bowler and to learn how to play the thing.

25

On the long train wrong drain paddle cracking wires, all scratching the burn-sparks across the Laudenum night-tunnels, screeching the rails with aspic defiance, Firk and the stone philosophic rolling at the end of the day to the rallying relay, the rasping, the gasping, the never ending, opus of folk-joking joik-foiking, the babble of babel's Uncle Bob, swifting up to La Stade Nationale, stuck like a boil on the dark far north-north-west of the lauded numb of the capitalizing capitol and like a stolen rhone left leaping out the windows of wisdom, left sleeping out the chicken scratch of random and leaningmess, keeningfess, the fusion of mixed up confusion on the petty union, the pretty onion, the maiden in armour striking down the guard of the van and the tambourine man himself up there swinging like they'd never swung on the rung in this or any other time. A present from Sophocles, priced beyond reason of the season, the greens and the goodness, the dance and the dreams of the beatific scene. There up on the stage, the tiny figure playing his guitar and oh for those skipping reels of rhyme to find in refuge. They bought some beers in the brief interval that led to the world of petty heartbreak and heartache, the songs falling softly like amplified april showers in the course of spring. The be-bearded hippy at his side told a tale, implausibly the ragged end of the lung being passed, first the piss-poor beer by the black forest duo sat alongside, waking on the Thursday to the news in deepest deutschland, driving two days with naught but a pack of papers and a tonne of mystic that they roll and roll and roll again, passing up the line while telling of the times of Albert's free trade festival hall and Ernie being sat behind the judas as the cry came out, you're a liar, and the times just kept on changing while the time itself stands still and spends just one too many of its mornings so many thousands of miles behind the lines, outside the gates and down on the street, as the lady with the saddest eyes has but too many visions and you soon get the picture that the whole of the floating soaring world black forests its way through the camper van's night ride to eternity, to the end of the endless, to the last of every breath of every encored chord of the ceaseless night and walking wildly out into the stoner's moon, the rattle and spack, the all-but empty, thirsty, careering the corners and swerving the ways, still reeling, still rolling, still rollicking on the final fumes as the barbarian beards of Eddie and Ernie blast their volks-wheels for the border once again.

26

They'd stepped down from the 30, hot on the heels of some woman who'd been sitting on the lower deck as they smoked away on the top, still agush of the rush but desperate for the flat to kip in. The journey back had been long and as they'd still been drinking much of the way, both were in need of relief. While the wasteland would have made a nifty pit-stop, the woman had already shot off at speed across there towards the towers, so instead they went through the partially-lit patch of run-down shop fronts, still ranting, still raving still wailing away and still half-stoned on the back of the black forest's best.

Although she'd taken the unlit shortcut, the woman was still standing waiting in the lift lobby, as grim as it always was, with its yellow-peeling paintwork and ever present stench of piss. Wherever the lift had been making its way from, it was taking its usual, pondering time but it was at least working and they were all grateful for that. The three of them waited for a little longer before it finally pinged as if breathing its last and the doors groaned to life as if being woken with a hangover. Built for the purpose of getting eighty flats'-worth of furniture up twenty floors, the lifts were wide and deep, capable of stacking three sofas and a sideboard full of gin. But it had probably suffered a hernia soon after that first batch of tenants moved in and had spent the next twenty-five years failing everyone who tried to rely on it. Three floors from the ultimate pain of the penthouse, Sophocles and Franny had little other option.

The woman hovered at the controls and took charge of beaming them all up, while Fircle and Sophocles slunk to the back. They all remained silent, as people generally do in lifts, so it was handy that she pressed 17 as she hadn't bothered to ask either of them which floor they wanted and it saved one of the brothers having to raise up off the wall and press it themselves.

Slowly the three ascended, the wires ringing and tiring from the strain. By the morning, it would be out-of-order again and they'd be taking the stairs. After what seemed like a life of Sundays, they finally jolted to the holt of the halt. At two in the morning, all the three of them wanted was to be back inside a warm room and by then Fircle's bladder was fit to burst, but the woman had already placed herself front and centre, impatient for the doors to grind open once again. As they finally did, she pushed herself through the gap before they were even half-way apart, and she was out, frantically looking from door to door, panicked beyond terror itself, looking to run or to hide or to scream or to cry. Fircle felt all the life and joy drain out through his boots and drop the seventeen floors through the lift shaft. Oh, dear god.

The late bus across Laudenum to the East of the End. Never a pretty affair. End of the line, she gets off, followed by two young men that she doesn't know. Perhaps foolishly, she makes a dash across the dark of the wasteland, heading for Tower 3. A shortcut of shadows and demons, but she makes it to the lobby safely. The lift is working but it takes forever to climb down just four floors. And then the two men are behind her, sauntering in the way of the entrance leading back to the wasteland and the shuttered shops. The only other way out, towards the stairs, also leads to what was laughingly called the 'utilities zone' a dumping ground for broken furniture, piss-stained mattresses and the bins big enough to dump a body in. Neither is an option. Just get home. The lift comes but they get in with her, not allowing her the space to breathe. She'd pressed 17 - maybe it was her floor or maybe she'd hoped that by heading towards the top that they'd be getting off lower down, maybe she didn't want them to know where she lived and picked a floor, any floor, at random. But they hadn't moved. Neither was going to get off anywhere other than where she was going.

As the brothers came out of the lift, the terrified woman was still standing in the centre of the 17th floor lobby, her eyes wild with unhidden fear at what was happening, her head turning from door to door, wondering whether to knock or to scream. The brothers, now fully aware of her fears and suddenly sober, dashed for their own door, Sophocles scrambling for his keys. Fircle was shaking. His brother may well have been doing the same but both were too stammered to speak. They'd been so engrossed in their own existence that neither had considered the impact that jumping in a lift with a lone woman could have. Fircle felt sick to the bottom of his stomach. It was the first inkling he got of what it is like to live as a woman in Laudenum, or anywhere else for that matter.

They left the pub around eleven as it was getting to the point where the short were going down under foot and you could no longer get to the bar. People were passing their money over heads to those at the front and hoping that what came back was what they'd shouted for. Fircle had called for three pints of black and a lager and got a trayful of whiskey shots in return, so it wasn't always bad news. The problem was, you never knew how long your luck could hold on to its widow's weaves and no one was ever getting any change back either. But getting out was harder than it at first appeared. While Lowen and Fircle were too long in the leg and had to force a route through the melee, Sophocles and his gaslight made it out the window. But instead of the head for the home, Lowen had heard tell of a party up in the Old Witch district that was bound to be worthy of their attention, so he claimed.

So they stopped at an offy for the offing and stepped out for what turned out to be a thousand-mile trek. By the time they were knocking on the door of a suspiciously quiet and unlit terrace two-up, most of the tins had been drunk and everyone was getting antsy. Lowen suggested they should knock anyway. It was a good job they did because it woke the only person who was in and after the time it had taken them to get there, missing midnight and starting to sober, someone needed to be found to foot the bill.

"Is Steve in? He was meant to be having a party."

"Nah, they all decided to go down to Aboukir Bay Square instead."

"What the fuck did they go down there for?"

"Fuck knows. Too many people an' all the pubs'll be shut."

"Mind if we come in and wait?"

It wasn't really a question as Lowen was already through the door by that point and the others were following him through to the lounge. Steve's house-mate, whoever he was, just went back to his bed and left them to it.

They sat for a while and waited as if something was going to happen. Franny put the telly on for a bit of the end of the New Year shows that were crawling towards their own final hurdle. Sophocles went first:

"You've got a really shit idea of a party, Lowen."

"Aw, man, I'm so sorry. Don't people be angry. Someone said he was having a party and..."

"Maybe he was," Franny interrupted, "just not here."

Fircle leaned across to his brother to fetch himself one of the last cans in the bag. As he did so, his foot clunked across something metal and he looked down to see what it was. Whoever had last sat there had tracked down to the centre of the city and left behind their rolling tin of Green Virgin. He picked it up, figuring to use someone else's navy than roll his own.

"Ooo, look what I've found." He held the open tin out into the middle so all could see inside, and perched to one side of the navy was a good and solid half-ounce of mysticised resin.

"Should we?" asked a tentative Lowen.

"Fuck it," said Sophocles, "he shouldn't have left it behind. Anyone could have found it."

"Anyone did," Franny added.

So Lowen began to roll and they passed it around. In the silence that followed, with a quick shared smirk, they rolled another. And so it continued until there was the sound of a key in the door. Lowen scrambled the tin back to Fircle who tossed it under his chair, hoping no one would suspect. But a thick fog and a perfumed scent had filled the room. A public school dormitory voice was asking who the eff they were while Steve, or whoever this one was, fetched his tin.

"Have you been smoking my gear?" he whined.

"Not us," confirmed Sophocles, his voice as honest as the days in winter are long, and all four stood, simultaneous, knowing that eviction wasn't far off.

"We were just waiting as someone said there was a party," Lowen started and the others realised he was a hairs breadth away from dropping them all in the shit. Sophocles and Franny were nearing the door but both Lowen and Fircle would be left cornered.

"Some others let us in about ten minutes ago," Franny threw in, "we've not long got here and they've not long left. You must have passed them on the road outside." This threw the collective entity that was 'Steve' and his mates, who now stood doing viable impressions of goldfish.

"There was no party," dormitory-boy finally said, indicating that they'd lost total grasp of the fact that someone had been smoking all their stuff.

"No party? Well, we'll all be off then," Lowen said, clapping his hands together and while jaws were dropped to the floor, the four of them marched out the door and into the night, suitably stoned for New Year on someone else's mystic.

28

Breaking through the residuals of a lower-level burn through, their location was on the twenty-fifth floor as no one escapes from the roof. Painting the grass green waterproofing round the swimming pool sized water-tanks with Dave the Spanner stood on top, twenty foot in the air, slapping on the paint with a mop. It was all he did. Day after day. Officially he was a plumber, hence his moniker, it being that all plumbers across all the twenty seven floors from 25 down to LG were "the Spanner" just as every electrician is always "the Sparks" and all the decorators are "the Paint". But Dave never left the tank room. He just painted it over and over in an increasingly thick-layered crust of green. He didn't even fix the leaks that he found there as someone else always came up to do that. He noted the fault, filled out the paperwork, completed the report and as one of the plumbers was more than capable of fixing it. But protocol decreed that somebody else always came up to do the actual work. He didn't mind. He got paid the same regardless.

For want of anything else to have them doing, Fircle and Chavez has been sent up with a two-inch brush a-piece to assist Dave in rolling his rock up the hill. There was meant to be a big move coming - there was always a big move coming - and the pair were being kept on to shift the furniture, despite the fact that they'd already mullered three cabinets and a couple of three-grand walnut desks. They knew the move wouldn't come before they both quit for college but so long as they were getting paid, no one seemed to care, least of all them.

Dave the Spanner never left the tank room. At least, not in the time they spent there. He was there when they arrived in the morning and still there when they left at the end of the day. He ate his lunch there, drank his tea from a flask that always seemed to be full and had no other reason to go anywhere else in the building or beyond it. There weren't any signs that he was sleeping in there but for all they knew he was doing just that. For all they knew, he had some secret space where he'd stowed a lifetime's supply of ham sandwiches and a sleeping bag.

The only perk Dave seemed to have was that he had a key for the roof to let the window cleaners out for their phantom drop. Apart from one of the sparks, they were the only ones allowed out there. Possibly because, according to the mental calculations that Chavez and Fircle had done, with a bit of a run-up and a good bit of power in the lift, a jumper could launch themselves far enough out to land smack-dab on the northbound platform of Laudenum Bridge Station. That was the level of boredom they had achieved while waiting for "the big move" that would never come. But as miserable as painting the tank room was, they got paid and the little newsagent on the walk down to the bridge sold sobranie drum. Possibly the finest pipe tobacco taste he'd yet discovered.

29

Epistrophus 'Hap' Stein occupied the third and fourth floors on the corner block of a wide open crossroads at the edge of the Jewish quarter. The writer and renowned music critic lived there with his wife Nora-Lee and their three daughters; Delia, Ruth and Esther, going down in age and height. What on earth Fircle was doing there was a mystery to him. Somehow he'd managed to get himself a weekend pass although he wasn't sure how or why, although Hap didn't seem to mind him too much.

The place was rammed with a lifetime's collation of ephemeric oddities that they'd been dragging around the world behind them: the books half-written and those half-read; masks from Azerbaijan tribes of young elders; the arts of tatumesque pianola players, whose fingerprints painted the wash of the walls; Picassed vases and dalied door-stops stepping at the stalls; focused sanity bridges of rollined cherry; the disques of francisco de goya gone in the wind and the wail and the weep and the woe. Piles of everything in just enough precarious balance which everyone's aunt could top hat and tails around but Fircle could only clunk upon. And just the endless mystery of how all the things of the world could possibly fit across these two floors.

Cynthia was known to the household like an old friend and she pulled Fircle through the door straight after her like a suitcase, as if he might get stolen before she could show him off. She was one of those people who finds 'things' and introduces them elsewhere. Fircle had only gone along because she'd spent a whole week in the office beating his brow until he gave way and agreed. The mistake he'd made was getting drawn into a conversation about olkies and folkies and far off worlds of which he knew nothing. From that point on, she was suckering him in and when then she found out that he played Dylan songs, his fate was formally sealed.

30

Hap was in the kitchen, prepping food for the coming gathering of the gathered: musicians, critics, writers, their husbands and wives would all turn up expecting to eat and they always ate well. He had a stack of king prawns, fresh from the frigid air of the docks, and was topping and tailing them to make them appear like credible food. To Fircle, the whole process looked like something from a horror film: the legs, the big black eyes, the innards, all deftly skimmed from the muscle, to be discarded.

"You know," Hap started, "I have this theory about the prawn, the eating of the prawn, that it's all about sex. You wanna go?" Hap offered the fully intact shellfish across to Fircle who was too busy gagging to accept.

"No? No worries. You can start on the dishes. You see, the prawn, when prepped and cleaned, is just a piece of muscle. Shiny when wet. Unpleasant to touch. But most important of all it's clean. 's what people want. All clean and cleared of all the grossities of life. You see, that's the intention people have in mind about sex. Clean in the sense that it is detached from its reality. And whatever their preference may be, since they can't get that from sex, they eat prawns instead."

Fircle was far too busy dry-retching into the sink, unable to find the plug, to listen. It was little Esther that saved him, showing him where the bar was that made the plug rise into the hole so the sink would fill.

"If the sink gets too full," she explained, "the weight of the water on the plug reaches the point where it's higher than the counterweight and the plug drops down. Stops us flooding the people downstairs."

For some reason, Esther's mini science lecture was a whole lot easier to stomach than Hap's theories on the prawn-fetish. So, he cleared the kitchen and then helped Nora-Lee clean the rest of the house, trying his best to appear domesticated. The three girls had wisely stayed out of the way while all this was going on, knowing of old that their mother's whirlwind approach, drawing everyone into the chaos of her cleaning, meant too much to do and too many feet underfoot to get it done. Around five, Fircle headed out with the three of them to get some treats before dropping into the Blockbusters so they'd be out of adult-way watching videos. Fircle and Delia had been earmarked for babysitting duties but that would just mean being on hand should the need arise, so they left Ruth and Esther in front of their telly and took the instruments and some cushions up on to the flat roof to play some music together. Around ten, Ruth came up to ask Delia if they could have a bedtime story and Fircle stayed behind trying to figure out the what-the-hell of finger-picking.

31

"You got to hold your fingers like so," she'd said, holding up her hand close to his face. Delia was trying to teach him to pick claw-hammer style, she on the banjo and he on the big dreadnought guitar of Hap's.

It'd kicked off the night before, as Fircle, the family and Cyn all squeezed up around the dinner table. They'd been listening to Hap tell them all he could about everything of the Village when he'd lived there - the bars, the folk clubs, the jazz joints long gone when the money fell out the door. And as the folk and blues singers came and went, eventually Fircle's hero, Dylan, came up.

"O, Fircle loves Bob Dylan," Cynthia told them, "Even plays some of his songs. He was telling me about it all only yesterday."

"That right, Fircle? Maybe you could give us a tune."

"Oh, yes, Fircle. Give us one of your Bob Dylan songs." Hap could never really tell with Cyn whether she was genuinely enthusiastic about one of her 'finds' or just taking the piss but he didn't mind either way as it was always good fun finding out. Fircle guessed he didn't have the best of voices, as no one had ever willingly asked him to sing but he didn't really get just how out of tune and off key he could get. But they were all happy and laughing and egging him on and Hap was getting his big ol' dreadnought down from the wall hanger and passing it over, he just went along for the ride and hope no one laughed. The guitar was a beautiful thing to behold and felt like wonder as he sat it across his knee.

"All tuned and ready to roll," Hap told him as he sat back down. Fircle strummed out a couple to tentative chords, then fetched a pick out of his shirt pocket. He tried a little run, just to get himself accustomed to the size of the instrument, before running into a strummed-out version of Dylan's *Don't Think Twice* then, at the final turnaround, dragged the tempo down to a near standstill to run it into two verses, the only two verses that he'd actually completed, from one of his own pieces.

"My man, that line, 'is your death in vain', that's one truly dark take on the blues."

"So, how does it end?" Nora-Lee asked, picking up on the fact that it didn't seem finished, "does she die or does the narrator talk her out of it?"

"Er... well... yeah. I'm not too sure how to end it. It feels like she should be saved but, like, that might be a bit of a cop-out. Like, my heart wants to save her but my head is saying that if I do, then it's like I'm saying everything that the guy does to her is okay, because there's someone there to sort it all out and pick up the pieces. And it changes the emphasis as well, from him as the villain and the girl as the victim, to it all being about the singer as the hero."

"Breaks my heart to say it," Hap said after a moment's pause for thought, "but you gotta be true, Fircle. And sometimes what's true ain't always what's good. Show life as it is."

"Not as you want it to be."

"Exactly. Say, maybe since you've entertained us, we should return the compliment."

Fircle stood to hand the precious Gibson back to him but Hap just leaned back in his chair.

"Not me, brother, my singing days, if I ever had any, are long behind me," and he held up his hands to bar the way, "pass it over to Delia."

"Aw, Pa..." But she took it anyway and nestled it awkwardly on her lap. For a moment, Fircle thought she was going to roll out a version of *Frere Jacques* or maybe *Kumbaya* but that idea didn't last too long.

"Sorry, it's not my usual instrument," she apologised before diving into the many verses of *The Cruel Ship's Carpenter*. Fircle didn't know the tune, could barely follow the chords and was mystified by the movement of her fingers as they plucked and picked with wild abandon.

"I bet you can't match that, Fircle!" cried Cyn at the end, after they'd all watched on in wonder.

"Match it? I'd have to work out what Delia was doing first. That was unreal!"

"Naw. I just had good teachers is all."
He looked to Hap as Delia stood up to hang the guitar back on the wall.

"Not me," he confessed, "I taught her some basics but most of it she's picked up from guys in the clubs. Tags along most nights when I'm out. Watches up close to see what they do and pesters the jesus out of the guys to show her what they know."

"I don't usually play much guitar," Delia told them all, as if trying to excuse the errors that none of them except maybe Hap, were skilled enough to hear, "I prefer to play the banjo. Sits on my lap easier and I like that big ringing sound you get. If you want, I'll try to show you some things."

Fircle nodded, his face flushed at the meagerness of his own abilities.

"Yeah. That'd be so cool."

32

When they woke, it was in the cold, Sunday-hours of the early morning. Nora-Lee had been up and thrown some blankets over the pair of them as they lay like spoons, the cushions for pillows, Delia's arm wrapped over him and tucked in against his chest. She thought it sweet that they'd both gone to sleep with still their boots on. The pair huddled up to each other, against the chill air, for a little while longer but as the light began to crease the sky, Delia got him up and moving to show him the view across her section of the city. Above a low-lying morning mist you could see all the way up to Republic Hill across to the north. He'd never seen that side of Laudenum before, never been this far north of the river. It was unlike everything of the city he knew - a strange new world beyond the dust and the bustle, beyond the parades of buy-what-you-want and the desperate beggars in need of some salvation, where the city itself seemed to have disappeared somewhere behind, somewhere into a past of his life that no longer existed, no longer mattered.

And so she toured him around the rooftop, looking out across the wonders of Laudenum, both draped in the blankets that Nora-Lee had brought. While the high-rise view from Tower 3 in Candlewick always gloried in the smog-orange glow, the simplicity of looking out on a morning, seeing into the treetops, the traffic just below but at the same time being above it all, was something magical.

Nora-Lee brought up freshly-made coffee for them in huge, continental-style mugs the size of a child's head, a luxury he'd only ever seen in French movies. The three of them stood, drinking slowly, as the day began to rise and the traffic to build.

"It's lovely up her on a Sunday," Nora-Lee said, breaking through their silent contemplation. They all felt the same.

"Have you slept?" her daughter asked.

"Of course not."

It was abrupt, but not angry, short, but not sharp. "You know exactly why" she was saying. Delia understood and blushed. Fircle was busy staring out at the city and missed the whole, brief, conversation. Delia explained later just how close to the wind he'd sailed by both of them staying up there on the roof through the night and sleeping there cuddled up to her, regardless of how fully-dressed they were, or of who was cuddling whom and the fact that they'd not even so much as kissed, or that her mother had probably spent most of the night listening below on the steps until she was sure they both were asleep and that all they'd been doing was talking and playing music. As they all turned and headed back over to the pile of cushions and instruments, Fircle could hear Nora-Lee whispering something.

"Psst," she'd said, "don't give daddy a heart attack. Let Fircle have his jumper back before we go down."

33

"You know, son, I think my eldest, Delia, has taken a shine to you. I don't know why. Maybe it's you playing guitar or maybe it's the life you might've seen. Now I'm not gonna tell you how to live your life, but tomorrow, you'll be gone again is all I'm saying."

He took the hint, even 'tho it wasn't a hint, and while what little time was left of that Sunday they'd spent in each other's company, both did their best to keep it on a low enough profile to keep her dad from needing to give him the talk.

But even if he hadn't given it to Fircle, he'd certainly given it to Delia, and Nora-Lee had also been squarely put in her place for even thinking such sentimental thoughts. For her, it was just two innocent kids falling for each other in the way young teens will do. So maybe Delia was a little more taken with her new friend than she otherwise would be with someone that she knew more regularly, but Nora-Lee knew such things don't often last and that, so long as she kept an eye on things to make sure nothing went any further than it should at their ages, it would all be okay.

But for Hap it was a different matter. His eldest daughter, only just coming up for fifteen, and a boy who seemed to have travelled around one too many blocks for his own good, himself pushing seventeen and barely known by any of them and there she was, all doe-eyed and loved-up over a solemn stranger. Hap made it clear that although they'd all enjoyed having Fircle stop by for the weekend and that he looked forward to hear how his songwriting progressed, he wouldn't be coming back any time soon. By which time he hoped that his daughter would have moved on, finished her education and maybe even settled down, it would be that long a time away.

In the weeks that followed, Fircle tried calling a couple of times and while he had a long heart-to-heart with her mother, he never got to speak to Delia again and the letter he wrote her at the end of that summer, telling her that he'd soon be just a stone's throw away to the north, went unanswered and most likely unread by anyone but Hap.

34

Slumped for shelter from the storm in a burnt-out bus-stop, the rain lashing what's left of the walls, collar turned up 'gainst night's grief-struck heart, no one calling 'come in' to save him from another lifetime or take him where it's safe and warm. No steel-eyed men fighting for truth or dishonour and not a lonesome undertaker in sight to cry, as there always should be on such nights of busy plunder. Just the rain and the high cold wind matting his clothes against his skin at 2am. As ever and always at times like this and that, he was shit-faced drunk, barely able to stand and broken of the soul. They'd pulled him out of the club before he made a scene and pointed him in the general direction of home. With no more trains, he careened the streets out to the Aboukir Bay roundabout, the Grand Central Station of the elusive night buses.

The Night Bus. Long run ritual of the damned and the late shift and the lushed-up drunks looking to make it home, as unpleasant in the world of the broken souls as the displaced spinal cartilage that the hours of rattling seats would bring on, with the choice between fists and fat leeches the length of the top deck and the drunken poverty below, with the workers winding home and those too far gone to negotiate the stairs. Fircle hadn't even been able to negotiate his fare and in the end the driver just waved him on to sit with all the other wastes of life on his mobile drunk-tank. Other than the stairs, there was little to choose between the flight from the fight or the uremic taint of the stained suit sat at his side, clutching an open can of special while trying to relight the stub of a butt-sucked roll-up held in the grip of his crusted lips, face pockmarked, nose variously split and broken, the cracked alcoholic veins revealed on his cheekbones like bloody rivers marked on the surface of Mars.

"Light 'iss for uz," he asked, turning to Fircle and trying to pass what was left of the smoke and his disposable lighter across.

"Sorry, I don't," Fircle lied in reply.

"Cunt," the man muttered, not even remotely under his breath. A woman took time to tut. He called her the same but louder.

Fircle started looking forward to a long trek of endless abuse, but after about half an hour the lower deck briefly cleared and the man moved up to the back and flaked out across the long bench seat. A woman who was still sat in the corner moved herself away from his rotting feet and had to remain standing for the rest of her journey.

There's something magical about buses after dark. As a kid, maybe it was just about being up after the sun had left the streets, being up late and out of the house, and then, as an adult, there's the thrill of heading out to life and the lights and a night full of promise. But that's not the Night Bus: the promises have all been broken, the kebab cutters are exhausted and fat still cakes their faces, the cleaners are sweat-stained and weary, the drunks covered in the contents of their kidneys, and everyone is cold and miserable for the three long hours it takes to circle the suburbs, Fircle dragging himself all the way back to Tombstone, pennilessly contemplating another hour's walk before even considering the prospect of closing his eyes, his headache building, the hangover growing, the thirst increasing. And cold to the bone in his wet clothes.

MAELSTROM

35

He never did handle change that well. Ma would be reminding him of that right up until the day she died. Changing jobs, homes, schools or whatever it was, would leave him reeling in the wreckage of his mind. Starting again in Maelstrom was no different. While they were all in much the same situation, all starting again having escaped from institutions where they didn't fully fit, he was trying to find an identity for the first time, after years of primal indoctrination in a place he spent his time alternately trying to escape from or burn down. But what was good was that he now had money in the pocket. Not much, but money none the less.

For the first month, he spent what he had on rolling navy, coffee and pints of black. His free time was spent smoking without end and guzzling back the java in the institute's canteen. The closest he came to eating was spending lunch breaks in The Hangman's Tree, the pub that sat so conveniently right across from the front gates. Most only went there once in a while but Fircle made himself a feature. Once safely sat in there, he would smoke and drink without stopping for breath until they all rose to return for the afternoon sessions.

It wasn't healthy but it was the best disguise that he had from the reality of talking to people that had all their own hidden agendas and secret histories and seemed to know each other from old. Before, in school, no one had anything hidden or worth hiding. As much as they tried, the uniformity of their existence had made them unmatched as zombie'd drones: pubescent, testosterone-laden boys all desperate to be held in the arms of someone, they all knew each other by scent and obscenity, knew each other's cheapest thrill and most tedious fantasy. But here he found something new - women for a start. Women who would talk to him, sit next to him even, walk with him to the train and ask him who he was and what he wanted out of life - and all without needing to be drinking or drunk. Such a state of being was an unknown world, a terrifying world where you had to think before anything you did or said. While his new compadres seemed to have mastered the rudiments long before, his years of incarceration had left him with a gaping void in his social skills. So as a defence, he chuffed at the smokes, puffed at the balkan drum in his pipe, shrouded up a cloud around and drank without mercy.

Not eating was nothing new. It had happened when he'd first set eyes on Eclipse Romain and now it was happening again when he first met Pendle Scope. A year older than most of them, she'd dropped out of school and dropped back in on a whim. She'd read books he'd never heard of, knew the music he'd started listening to like she'd heard it in the womb and had seen more of life than most of them ever knew existed. Everything he thought he knew, she knew already and in better detail and with a clearer grasp of how it all stood in the grand and gratuitous schemes of the omniverse.

Short and with a shock of bright orange hair, she greeted him as a fellow human being facing the same cruel world as she was, no longer just cannon-fodder to be fed through the meat-grinder but a person with a point and a purpose. And everything was right then in the world again, except... Pendle had picked up the signals loud and clear when they first sat in the canteen and he'd bought her a coffee. Maybe it was just the cut of his jib or maybe the drool-dog slog of the hook in his desperate eye gave the game away. Either way, it dragged along for a little while, he limpet-like at her side wherever the chance found its way to his feet and she trying not to encourage him but also trying not to hurt his feelings. She found him full of the strangest thoughts that fell out across the page of his face. In the weird of his wit, she found herself a friend to lean across to in the struggles they both had in staying the course - he breaking free from his incarceration, she, having once fled, trying to find a way back in. Eventually, she put him straight as soon as the chance arose, telling him all about Pablo Cortez who she'd been with for years but who was currently evading life's conscription at Birmidland Central, calculating the memory span of the stickleback. At some point, Pendle intended to join him there.

So Fircle smoked and drank and didn't eat in sorrow because he'd learnt the lash and limping truth of eternity, that forever in the elastic grin of space and time, there will always be a Pablo Cortez in melancholy's chamber waiting to punch him in the kidneys.

36

Bloated oafish goldfish mouth in a circle-spiral decline, filled refilled rescinding into stupors where no resuscitation holds more than a brief encounter with the breath of a vomit-coated tongue, the whisky'd stain now hid beneath the virtue of its cuddling bile, the rat's arse of fag ash burnt to sulphur-cinder the shot-blood eyes. Slumped like carrion in the corner, mocked and misused and left for the dead of the day to pick clean all packets and pockets of the worthy bone china memories of yesterday's dose of luck, the bundled berries plucked for ripe and shamble. Dribbling from the side of the mouth, the right of your face imprinted with a handbag zipper, snoring. They'll be lucky if there is no stain to the carpet, lucky if they can get you to leave before the dawn. You'll be dumped outside, reeking of booze and puke, sweating out your urine, desperate for love and comfort, for another bottle to clutch, sitting on neighbours' doorsteps wishing to find a face to fill the aching hole, the missing piece, the emptiness inside. But, just another bottle, dear god, to fight and feed this bile-burnt throat fiesta.

37

Eventually, we have to face the squalid remains of breakfast and stagger the detritus of absolution's far off pity. So it was with Fircle. For weeks he'd been struggling with the combined thrust of a lack of food and a lungful of smoke. When he wasn't so drunk that he passed out in the afternoon lectures, he was outside the building dry-retching into the bushes. He had little concept of whatever he was meant to be doing, had no grasp of even decent indecency and was gaining a worse reputation than even Sophocles when he'd been there. His brother had at least had the dignity not to drool out the side of his mouth and snore when he lost all consciousness. So it fell to Clifton Patrick to break the news. Fircle would have preferred it if it had been Leon Lenin doing the deed. With Leon he could at least confide the horrors of existence, knowing that that man had seen into the abyss for himself. But Clifton... he just seemed too embarrassed at the prospect of talking to one of his students about anything other than Etruscan Logistics.

They called him in on a Wednesday morning, straight after Modified Semantics, when he was still free all afternoon but before he'd had the chance to retreat to the safety of The Hangman.

"So..." Clifton paused. A long pause because he didn't really know where to start, where he was going, or how any of this would end. Fircle started to fidget and took out his navy to roll a smoke to give his hands something to do. Clifton frowned so he stuffed it all back into his pocket.

"So. We've been talking. Mr Ashmolean and myself, about how you're managing things so far."

"It's going fine. I like it here."

"Yes. Er..." and Clifton's face went red with blatant embarrassment, "you... er... seem to be enjoying The Hangman's Tree a little more."

"It's where we go for lunch. We all go in there."

"Yes... Lunch..." and there was another long pause, "You... er... seem to be having a lot of purely liquid lunches. Now I know your brother had something of a reputation as a rebel when he was here and it's quite natural for the young to want to rebel against the world. I was once a young rebel myself... but we... er... we'd hate to see you heading along the same path. And technically, you are still underage, so you shouldn't be drinking at all."

Fircle had no comeback. At that point Sophocles and Lowen, both of whom were ex-students of Clifton's, had taken up residence in a cold-water caravan on a farm and we're surviving on the meagre wages of fruit pickers. He sagged in resignation, expecting at any moment to get his marching orders. Instead, he discovered a truth that runs across education in the western world: students equal money and kicking one out for even the worst atrocity means giving an explanation to the accountants.

"We'd rather not lose you. Mary even said you've made some very valuable contributions... when you've been awake."

Everyone loved Mary. She taught books, dressed like a child of love in flowing, flowery skirts, spoke like she was stoned and had long red hair that seemed to reach down to the floor. Fircle would be alert enough to say a few words at the start of her classes, and then, as he sank into a stupor, would rest his head on his hands and fall asleep dreamily to her soft, kind face.

But, hell's teeth, if Mary thought he'd done something of value, that was reason enough to cut out at least some of the drinking, at least on a Thursday before her lessons.

Fircle walked out of the room and rolled a navy, having given all the right and relevant promises. He looked straight down the path towards the gates, beyond which he could see the opening door of the pub.

"Not today," he thought and headed off in the direction of the canteen, unless someone else happened to be heading that way.

38

In all his need to belong to something, to somewhere,
Fircle never embraced anything so completely as he did
the march of his indulgence in the wonders of Uncle
Bob. From the first few bars of the Greatest Hits album
that Pop had laid on him, he was hooked. His once
shorn locks grown out into a wild and woolly mass, he
talked Ma into ordering him some suede cowboy boots
and everything he wore was worn-in denim, with the
exception of his button-up corduroy cap. As skinny as a
rake, he looked like a matchstick painted faded blue, he
carried note pads of poems and songs wherever he went,
rolling his gangling frame into a loping gait, a copy of
Woody's *Bound for Glory* in his jacket pocket.

While his phases as a skinhead and mod were
attempts to be a part of a community, when he became a
figure of folk it was finally to find himself, so that when
anyone spied him from a distance they knew exactly
who it was. And once he looked the part he sought to act
it as well. He got the folks to buy him a guitar and one of
his neighbours, Levon Hunke, showed him a few simple
chords to get him started. He would strum the strains out
of the tambourine man's patience, roaring out the
songbirds of the south into early migration.

His trip to college became an exercise in riding the
rails. He would roll a smoke, navy stowed in his top
pocket, leaning against a wall as he sat on the floor
reading his Woody Guthrie or writing songs he couldn't
sing. When arriving at a station he would jump from the
train while it was still rolling, perfecting a smooth

transitional landing, like the hobos of old, like Kerouac in San Francisco, so he wouldn't fall on his face. Everything he did was an attempt to compound the cool of his dylanesque persona, to show the world that this is who he finally was.

39

Somewhere off in the night, the music pelted out a pogrom of popular hits and wild, rollicking indie, bursting out through the open windows to fall across the whole valley and into the setting of the summer's sons. Many of them were laid out on the garden's grasp in little groups, parlaying the parlance, the sultry boys and pouting girls, the lip-glossed and the over-after-shaved, the roasted and dog-bitten and the sold.

Limerick was welding the mystic, his agile fingers seemingly able to work multiple wonders as if in the thrall of a mighty machine. Passing the peas, he straight-out started another, knowing that the bogart would soon arise somewhere beneath the stars and that Fircle, Nancy and he could burn the other to the roach betwixt themselves should the need come to pass.

While her boyfriend was stiff as a board, Nancy Whiskey knew there was good value to be found in being kippered and understood the joy of the big beyond. Like Limerick, she also knew when enough was enough and could pace herself through the course of events. Fircle, however, was finding it increasingly difficult to stage-manage his intakes, hence the bottle of mezcal that he now sprang from his pocket. His new discovery had fallen to the lap of his land through the yahey letters of the burrowed bill and the Big Bin of Oddities off-licence that had opened just yards from his stationed stop. While the others declined, Fircle took a big lug and winced.

"Yikes, that's mighty stuff."

"What's that in the bottom..? Oh, god, it's a caterpillar!"

Limerick took the bottle to confirm their suspicions.

"It's the worm," Fircle explained to Nancy's initial exclaim, "it lives in the cactus, eating at the flesh but basically it's storing up concentrated mescaline in its body. When you've finished the bottle, you eat the worm to divine the Mexican visions."

"I thought you were a vegetarian."

"Yeah, that's true. But to be honest, I don't even think I'd have the stomach to eat it even if I did eat meat."

"You are fucking mental if you're eating that," Limerick told him, "why don't you have a puff of the mystic instead. It's quality Angolan Red. Nothing beats it."

Fircle took a share and propped up on his elbows to watch for the darkening sky.

"This world is my ceaseless dream," he murmured.

40

Nancy Whiskey was small enough to fit in your pocket and fierce enough to tear out your spine if you were dumb enough to try. She took no fools as prisoner but left them out in the ditch of the highway gasping for clemency like a futile arcade stop sign, having herself having seen of all the nine wonders and the ten thousand things that are known to the Dao. She took no fools and loved the rest, carried them with her, like precious fragile bird's eggs saved to birth the future. None of them understood how she valued the things that she did as she carried the devices of freedom and will within so many prism-chamber locks that none could but divine or to whisper. But they all loved her because she knew what was held in store and laid the dark of the world as bare before them as she was ever to be allowed.

If she spoke they listened-intent. If she sat so still and silent, she was taking every sound into her delicate ears filling her head with every thought. She heard everything, like a mother aware of the stones of the earth. If needed, she would advise, quietly, without judgement, without treachery or spurs. She carried them in their dreams in the waves of hope they held so dear, cherished in her hands so prematurely gottonic. Limerick, Norma Wisdom, Fircle, the genuine wren, the reverendess Al Green, all of them, even the twine of Ruby Shoesday, despite her adherence to the will of Harvard, could find herself in carriage.

But Nancy also held in her head so many future visions of future times, saw them fall, stumble, win, fail and she would tell them the stairs to avoid, the bamboo spit pit traps and the weak-tea flops to ditch in the switch. Her eyes would see the inglory rusted in decades of dance and dervish whirl, in the frantic semantic of oblique and basquiat fusions; the vitriolic staunch of non-clomentic protocols left in the bizarre and cordiality; the tang of the blowfish failed and traced above. And she had also seen the manner of Fircle's death.

41

It felt like he spent most of his time either on trains or waiting for them. He didn't mind. Lowen had laid the Book of Woody on him and travelling in the comfort of smoking class had become his equivalent of riding the rails. He would sit on the platform, just out of the rain, hat pulled down over his eyes, raggedy clothes, old army bag of books and notepads and a gently burning roll-up hanging from his lower lip, with "I'm a ramblin' man rollin' round from town to town" ringing on in his ears. Playing the part of pretending himself the hobo, he rode on his student-pass rails from home to Maelstrom day after day, him and his hipstered friend and maybe a little mystic for company.

Some days, Roula would join them, and maybe Kruger Luger also. In the peak of the summer, as everyone's money began to run dry, Limerick taught himself to roll a smoke as thin as a matchstick, with maybe only two or three strands of navy for taste. He kept what he had for sharing with Fircle, sometimes Roula who was always free with cigarettes when she had them. Kruger had a habit of demanding to roll his own, always fat, always plenty, always a near-empty tin to last Limerick the night. That fucker could fit a whole half-ounce of navy in a single rizla. All three took to checking for Kruger so they could squirrel the goods before he boarded.

So Kruger took on the taste for the george stubbs that always littered the carriage floor. Both Limerick and Roula drew the line right there and although Fircle had started out raiding the ashtrays at home, once he had the money for his own, or companions that would flash the ash, he avoided the practice in general. It had bad associations. He'd seen his nan unraveling the butts of her rollies as she tried to eek out the weeks ration a little further. The bastard she'd married always had to have plenty in his own tin of Green Virgin, so she made do with the scraps to avoid him punching her down the stairs again.

42

He was intrigued.

"I can't tell you that," she confided, but like a fool he pressed and pressed til she had no will to give beneath the graceless sky.

"I'll tell you some," she said, "not all of it. Not... Some of it wasn't nice at all. It's... I... I saw how... I saw how you die. In my dream, I saw how you die."

"Ya-hey! That's my kinda dream," he joked, hoping to use a little levity to put her at her ease and then maybe she'd be a little more forthcoming, because, like... this wasn't just anyone... this was Nancy Whiskey having dreams about him. Nancy Whiskey! Their very own delphic sprite. But she didn't laugh and she didn't smile.

"I dreamt about you and... I saw you die."

"If you're gonna tell me I get shot in the crossfire by a load of jealous women at the age of 97, I can handle it. I have the same fanta... sorry... 'dream' myself."

This time she did laugh.

"You should be so lucky," she added. Then there was a pause.

"Was I raising the red flag over parliament?" He laughed and again she didn't. The pause continued and all it needed was the monochromatic ticking of a giant clock to be a truly cinematic moment in either of their lives. But there wasn't one. They were alone in a corner of the canteen, away from the others that they usually sat with and occasionally one of those would look over towards the pair and wonder what the secret was all about.

"It's not nice," she said again, "I saw how you kill yourself."

A voice came into his head, one that he'd been hearing since he first understood the meaning of death:

"He hanged himself," the voice always said, matter of fact, almost a taunt, almost an instruction, it never being clear exactly which. As ever it drifted in and out, barely touching the sides. For years it had been a voice as clear as anyone speaking next to him, but he had managed to internalise it, to take it inside so it no longer spoke through his ears but lived instead like a thought in his head. While death-dreams are common and you pay them no mind, Nancy didn't have just any dreams. She saw things plain as day and when they spoke you took their heed.

They sat still closer, looking straight at one another, the video still on pause, the clock still ticking as still time still stood still on its stilts.

"Christ," he thought, "I've never looked into a woman's eyes so deep for so long."

"Hanging?" He eventually asked, knowing what the voice had for years been telling him.

"No. It was... it was horrible."

"Horrible?" Fircle laughed nervously, "How horrible is horrible?"

"Really. Really... quite... disturbingly horrible... Don't do this but... if you think of the most horrible way a person could die by suicide, it was worse than that. Far worse."

Fircle's mind went to the Buddhist monks setting themselves ablaze during the Vietnam War. That was about as worse as he could get at such short notice. Her eyes turned down:

"I shouldn't have told you."

"I'm glad you did," he'd said, "it's better to know than to not. And besides, I'm flattered. It's not often that I have women telling me they've been dreaming about me."

"It's not really that sort of dream," she said, raising an eyebrow.

"Look, I'll take what I can get. If a woman dreamt about throwing me in a cess-pit full of vomit to drown while being eaten alive by rabid piranhas, for me, that's as good as a snog behind the bike sheds."

Nancy Whiskey squeezed his hand with a smile and the pair of them went back over to where the others were just beginning to drag their heels towards the next session of Eugeniasticology.

She'd floated in as the summer sank to its knees and pleaded for the lord's redemption. As unforgiving as the autumn is, with its graceless tongue and it's open hand, it's failed romance with the sun would often bring in a puzzle on the waning tide. So it did that year, as Fircle and Limerick feigned embrace, not having seen each other since the July. And while Fircle had worked through the summer, shifting boxes of other people's money to & fro, Limerick had busied himself with matters of the heart and soul. Next to him in the canteen sat a woman dressed entirely in black with dark, ringlet curls that hung down like swirling flowers over her shoulders. While Limerick was his usual live-wire of flailing, excited arms, wild eyes and meandering, addled stories, Elle was all quiet eyes and tactical avoidance, although it was sheerly clear that she was deeply in love with him.

"So, all we got to do now is get you fixed up, get you all loved-up for the winter, eh, Fircle? Wha' about it Roula? You'd go out with him, eh?"

"Fircle? I do have some standards, thank you very much."

"Yeah, but they're pretty low."

"As low as they are, Limerick, they're not THAT low. I wouldn't touch *either* of you with someone else's bargepole."

Fircle laughed. Elle laughed. Roula laughed, sitting smug. She had a quick Yiddish wit, master of the slung-back take-down that she could play like a fiddle.

Limerick would fall for it every time and never once did he ever get the better of her. But while he was listening and laughing, Fircle had noticed on that first return to the cauldron someone new, sitting up by the pillars with the retake-crew, some of them like Lavender back for maybe the second or third time around. She had a quiet smile, equally quiet eyes, and was sipping at her coffee as if afraid it would tell.

There she sat like pristine an dream, the quake of matter's placid face shaking rock to ruble, from rubble to stubble, the stammer of the heart in a mark and the cor-blimey call of the sweet-love and luckless. Desperate wisdom, the Cyrillic stabat mater, the monster, the myth of the hundred blinded ogres limb-from-limbed by their adoring quarry. Pray you don't recover. Play you don't discover what warm welcome waits in the harms of shell-shocked mouthy grin. The cubits of uncommon flesh, the creosote of heavenly kingdoms crushed beneath jesuit sanctities and apposite postures as medici'd servants beckon their swill come fade. This is the law of the longing of the heart on a whispered whim, these times the taken tale dropped from the drop-kick dance to devour. Thus is the last long gasp of grief before the bellows beckons and werewolves wail their lupine armours. Such, if the wells of mermaids' memory serve us of our sins and the gracing grains of gavelled adoration is ought but the mockery of time, she sat like a jewel in the mysteries of Maelstrom, the whirlwind drawing out from the bleak seats but once the hapless hope of a happenstance so sweet, someone so honest. No one had seen her but he. No one had witnessed but the

drop of his jaw in the wonder that he wanted so much
now to know.

44

Corina Corina hailed from the moors but less was known. Her family had fled to the south for a reason she may never have spoken of and a question he failed consistent to ask or to talk. With her soft long locks an her boots an her socks she walked in the room as the girl from the north country, an angel of folk proportions written in songs passed down through mountain trails. In her herringbone coat, she smiled and it broke his heart into appalachian splinters.

Fircle couldn't but keep from looking and longing and as the autumn leaves turned to winter rain, he stood at the base of the Maelstrom College Tower and watched as she walked away. He felt the gullible of his inability to swallow threaten to stop his breath complete and as she took to the top of the steps, she turned to smile again. And she waved... Dear god she waved, just the slightest upturn of the wrist and a dance of the digits, but all was clear, dear god, was all so implausibly clear.

"I think she fancies me," said the lime of the Limerick at his side with a jolt of the elbow, while Fircle just goldfish gawped, "If you don't go after her, mate, I will."

As Corina stood in herself at the tops of the steppe, beginning to wonder if she was herself the fool, he took too much of a moment for the penny to drop. Then as much as he tried to stride with the porpoise of purpose, he clumsily clunked in his boots of Spanish suede to her side.

"I'm..."

"Oi, Corina, you coming?"

She looked down to where her friends were waiting and shouting and chuckled in a Yorkist brogue:

"You might've guessed, I'm Corina."

"Fircle," he said, "but you can call me whatever you like."

"I'll call you Fircle," she said with the slightest wrinkle of her nose, "I like Fircle."

45

By the time he'd fought his way through the waves of wade in the water to the bar and bought her a drink, she'd got herself a seat at the end of a window bench in the far distant corner.

"I did try to save you a spot at the end but I kept getting pushed farther and further along a bit more each time someone came over and now I'm barely clinging on."

"Thass fine," he said, putting down his pint and bending down to be heard but, damn, why did her friends have to be there as well? Did none of them have something better to do than this, to get themselves drunk on the last day of term before the Christmas break? His own crowd were across at the far side of the room by the door and he waved at them to acknowledge that he'd seen them and wasn't just being ignorant. Limerick was laughing and looking back at him and the laughter spread. Bastards, he would've thought, if Corina wasn't at that moment asking him something. Her voice was quiet and she wasn't so good at shouting above the rabble.

Pinned up against the wall with barely the boot-room for toe to heel, the only way they could speak is if he bent himself hairpin double at the waist. And where the college crowds had gathered, the table had been shunted further and farther towards the wall behind Corina as more and more crammed in, pinning her in her seat. Neither of them would be going anywhere anytime soon, unless the wall collapsed or they please crawled out their window. Out of the corner of his eye he saw Limerick snaking his way to the bar and as there was no chance of him getting back over there this side of empty, Fircle hollered, held up his pint of black and pointed. He got a thumbs up and then his mate made gestures that he assumed were a question as to what Corina wanted - basically it was the standard mime for drink followed by his hands shaping out a woman's curves. Fircle picked up her drink - a whiskey and orange. How in the name of the great lord fuck was Limerick supposed to know what that was? Fircle put it down. Bugger. Shouting was the only answer.

"Whiskey and orange!" he bellowed above the crowd of chatter, when an instant before, every soul in the pub had taken a pause in talking to have a sup. Such was the silence that you could actually hear the feint sound of the jukebox as a backdrop beneath him with Uncle Bob telling his lady-love to lay across his big brass bed. The wife and her world of wonders stopped to look, Fircle blushed and the landlord yelled:

"Bells alright for the lady?"

"Bells is good," Fircle hollered back.

"Bells is good," shouted most of the pub in piss-take response, at which the voices and the volume jumped and The Hangman thronged into chaos once again. Shortly after, two pints of black and a very large whiskey with a side of orange made their way along either side of the tables, one from Limerick and one courtesy of the landlord for giving him a laugh.

Corina was still smiling. He figured she couldn't be drunk as she was still talking fluent and was still on her first drink. She was telling him about moving south, something about her dad's work when some movement caught his doubled-over eyes. Somebody had stood.

"Quick, shift up, shift up."

Corina obliged and after he'd managed to squirm his feet out from the jam they were in and get his legs under the table, they finally managed to sit together and for what seemed like an age of Sundays they just sat grinning sideways at one another. He wanted so much to know what she was thinking, to tell her everything that was in his own head, but all that he could do was smile because of the smile that she was giving him. She giggled, happy in the intoxication of what? She'd barely touched her drinks but she was holding his hand, her face so close to his he could feel each flicker of her lashes against his own as Inuits spoke of love, their lips so close to barely touch, a hair's breadth, the softly perfumed scent of her skin and the warm glow from her lips that he could almost feel inside. And as if suddenly alone in the universe, beyond those sat at their table, beyond the crowded bar, beyond both her friends and his and the calls and the jeers and the whoops of wonder, they kissed. They kissed as if they would never stop, as if the world could end in that one moment and nothing would ever bring them to be apart.

46

So bounding arounding in the street-lit Maelstrom night strutting peacock, the cool, the fool, the half-cut drool, falling beyond the love-in-vain like the love-struck, dumb-struck, drunk on the adoring to be adored, oh hail the lord for this, oh hail the damned lord as the neon draped shadows of alleyways and underpasses disappear into the dreams of tomorrow, the phantoms of past immemorial times crashed out in the gutters of all eternity.

The Galleon's Slew being the pub of choice for the literary kicks crowd, the poet's and the posers and their princely goals, with the upstairs bar, all black-oak pews and glowing embers, was the perfect setting for the poetry readings that never took place there. Instead, you could sit & converse to the background drop of elusive duritti'd guitars piped out by the spike-haired gent behind the bar.

Fircle found them a table and rolled himself a navy while Corina Corina slipped up to the bar to get their drinks. She came back with a pint of black for him and a lush for herself. She drank it slow to keep her head, while Fircle drank fast to steady his nerves, and once he'd laid them to sleep, he drank further still to keep them that way.

Corina took his hand in hers across the table and just smiled. All quiet and dimpled-cheeks aglow. And he knew then that there was nothing better in the world than to be looked at by someone like that.

"Oi, oi, move along the pew."

Limerick moved into the space alongside Fircle and his muse sat herself opposite him. The two women looked at each other and nodded their greeting more than saying anything, with Corina still trying to extract herself from the fix of her smile.

"You two look 'appy," the lin mcgrin smirked and the pair both flushed, loosened their tangle of fingers and spoke them each to their drinks as if in hiding. Mystery solved in absence of the impossible rivers, the four then sat and chewed the fat of the land and the lamb until just shy of the closing bell.

The dirk of the firk and the lignum of the limerick were both due on the midnight train and would have to leave the ladies to the ladle's grip of Maelstrom to see themselves home. So the four then flew to the dash of the barrack station where they stood in their couple's to bid the price of their fare-the-wells.

Fircle pulled Corina in close with his overcoat wrapped at her sides for warmth in the devil of the decembered night. And oh, how still she smiled. And oh, how still the world could walk in the glory of the lords of love and besotted. And oh, in that brief moment of a wild blazing night-time, how could he ever forget as she pulled his face down to meet his and kissed him for what seemed an eternity, until the wail of the train's brakes signaled that the final sprint was close at hand.

47

Christmas Eve. A bitter Maelstrom wind pulling through every street, raking up the salt of winter into a blinding haze. Pop was on the prowl for a gift for his better half – his annual tradition of leaving it always to the last of minutes, the final chase to the line. For Fircle, what it meant was a ride into town, and for an opportunity to see his Corina. Beyond that nothing else mattered to him: Not Christmas; not a smoke; not even a quick couple of pints; Hell, not even the cold mattered. Not anymore. She was the kind of person you could spend a lifetime making mix-tapes for. Not just a bland splatter of current ways of screaming love! but damn! the important shit too, the sounds with meaning, *the Birth of the Cool*, *London Calling*, and he could hear her heart singing with his as *Love Minus Zero* rang out and rattled the wings of passing sparrows. She was the girl from the north country whose pretty little feet you'd shoe, she was Lisa Radley, the English rose and Johanna of the visions. And he just wanted to be her milkman of human kindness. Life was as good as the graces would ever let it be. It truly was the gravy of days.

So he strode like rode and made his way to someone else's haunt, The Wizard's Staff, somewhere he was fully unfamiliar with and somewhere packaged with revellers starting their evening proceedings early. Corina had said she'd be there early with one of her friends that she was meeting up with for a quick sherbet before Fircle got there, which was cool enough and in nervous jangled blast he shifted through to the bar and got himself a pint. Took a sup to settle and started searching. Although she'd said she'd be there early, no matter how deep into the dark corners he squeezed his frame there was no immediate sign of her. But that was cool as there was a good hour before calling time and an hour more before his lift back left. Everything fine and everything dandy like jim.

He waited a while longer in sight of the door before making another round of the routes towards tables in case he'd missed her but there was still no sign. Half-an-hour left. He bought another pint. It was difficult to not keep swigging when you're standing holding your glass, no one to speak to, no where to put it down, nothing to do with your mouth but drink. The tock ticked by. Time was called. He bought another pint. People started to empty out. He could see every corner and she definitely wasn't there and she hadn't come in with anyone. A half-dozen people were left at the bar, finishing drinks, known to the staff, and then there was Fircle with the best part of a pint left still to down. The landlord kept looking over disapproving. A few more bodies left. Then the door creaked gently open.

"We're closed!" the landlord shouted, as much at the man who stood in the doorway, desperate for another, as at Fircle who still hadn't finished his. He took the hint, downed the last half in one and left. She hadn't shown.

48

With the snow cleared back from the track and the trains finally running, Fircle was able to get back to his world and to take a break from the weak-long lock-in at The Wolf's Head. With no one able to get along the road to open the shops or the bank, Guido had been happily cashing cheques, knowing that his pub was the only place open for anyone to spend their money anyway. He was quids in both ways. In contrast, Corina hadn't been around to take any of his calls, however constant he made them, and he got the feeling that her mother was sick to the back of her teeth with giving him more of her daughter's excuses.

Their last conversation had been awkward, stilted, even difficult. She'd been explaining away why she'd stood him up for the second time on new year's eve, when they'd been due to meet once again in the Slew, this time without the baggage of others being present. One of her friends had gone into a tear-stained meltdown as her fella had dumped her like a bag of cats cast into the Medway and she'd spent the entire evening doing the consolation routine. It took her a while to get through the whole course of events and he'd just sat listening to the beautiful sound of her voice, hearing every gentle smile as she gave him a reason to believe. But there'd been that question at the start, the one that had nearly brought everything to an end.

"Fircle," she'd said, "do you think we're going out?" As a question, it was something that had never occurred in any of his meanderings that he'd ever have to find a decent answer for. Much later, he'd thought that maybe she was after something a bit more committal and concrete than what she actually got from him, but he'd been wrong-footed and the best he could manage after some stumbled stutters was:

"Well, yeah, if you like."

But then they'd carried on talking for another hour or so, which must have meant his answer, short and shambolic as it was, was okay. But since that call they'd not even said so much as a "howdy-do". Whatever had happened in the rest of the universe, he'd been locked down and trapped by four-foot snowdrifts, hustling for bread and coal and cashing so many cheques he could stay drunk for a week.

So finally he was able to bound his way up to the canteen, fully expecting to see her waiting for him with open arms at the door. The fact that she wasn't was a bit of a kicker but most of the others were there so he dived straight in to the old routine of coffee and drum. He regaled them with tales of the non-stop drinking that had gone down in The Wolf and Limerick looked genuinely gutted that he'd been staying with Elle, getting stoned and making love, while his mate was getting blitzed. So Fircle made himself busy chewing the fat and catching up with those who'd last seen him with his face buried in that of Corina and they wanted to know how it was going. He was so engrossed that he didn't even see her come in. It was Roula who drew his attention back to why he'd run up the hill in the first place.

"Isn't that you-know-who," she nudged. He looked up, at Roula puzzled, and then over to the table where

Corina often sat with her friends. There she was, at the head of the table, which made it easy for him to pull up a chair by her side.

He gave her a cheesy greeting and asked her endless questions. She answered quietly, without any real conviction that she was part of his conversation and instead of looking at him, she kept her eyes straight ahead, looking down the length of the table. Eventually, she and her friends all got up to leave. All except Fircle who was left sitting billy-no-mate, his crest fully fallen and lying in the fag-ash on the floor.

The day that followed followed much the same pattern as if it had been cut in the sweat shops of life's existence. Except her smile was back. She spoke less and he asked fewer questions but that oh so smile was there on her face again as she sat staring still straight ahead. But she spoke so much less, not a word in return that he hadn't prompted and not even a sideways glance to guess at his thoughts. This day she didn't even acknowledge him when he sat by her side. Just smiled, spoke to her friends and smiled. Knowing something that he didn't, or something he could never comprehend. Like a jester without a king, he sat awaiting an instruction that never came, and through his lunch he did exactly the same. He didn't eat and smoked in chains and for three days lived as the same. Silence. The smile. The laughter she shared with her friends as they walked away. After three days, he got the message.

49

So when first he found the fool, it beckoned with a glad-hand a-loft, cheeky minstrel in pied pie-eyed attire, the leavened bread of its gaze all handsome skew, all soon betrothen. It beckoned with a gladsome glue afloat, adrift in the mired tines and of tired mines, minds stuck in purgatoried despair, the happy honey of its golden voice calling through shades of Indian summer evenings and blessing as it does to the suffering of life in its arms and squeezing it into love itself, of spires high and lords afloat, the breeze in the sails and the lapping of the dawn.

Smokes gave him a home, as would later the lash of the lush and the soft roll of mystic when it opened its doors. As a side-bet on safety, he dodged the bullet of the ampersand's rush, trying instead to chase the shaken tail feather. But the loss of his equilibrium was such that he had to vomit through his eyeballs, dooming their prospects from the start, and blocking any flight to Mexico or Tunis. Whatever he tried to kill the dark fell a-foul of the dark's return and the abyssal plane, leaving him only the clasp of the rum for the comfort.

Limeroo did what the why that he could to keep the face of the Firk stoked with mystic, tempting and attempting to mellow his mood from the fault line functions of his fractured heart but it didn't seem to help. Nothing helps to the pitying self determined to throw itself down from the parapets of byron. He saw his friend sliding through the holes in the net, unable to wake from the walking death that he had made unto his own. He saw his friend fall into the river of the lost and sorrow, a young man bracken in tears and mezcal, longing for a raft but without holding the hands with which to grasp it.

Fircle would stuff his pipe with balkan drum and sit within a cloud of shadows. Coffees would be left for him but he wouldn't eat and only left his seat to join the others in The Hangman, where he would switch to the lynyrd limerick's navy rolls and drink the black until they made him stop. But deep as in their hearts they sang to overcome the jester's weakness, there seemed to be no way of shunting him out of the dereliction of his duty.

It was a situation helped and hindered in equal measure by Fircle's discovery of fool's gold. The mystique of the mystic would quiet his mind but it gave him room to think and to dwell. But the fire of the fool was that it let him dream through his waking moments and in these dreams he sat in the folds of her arms on summer days surrounded by the scent of roses and sweet perfumes of the east. While his mind ran tawdry psychedelic patterns as an act of normality, the brew of fool's gold infusion would softly hold his hand and pass him through the gates of love again as if all in the world was good with the gods once again.

Whatever name it went under, it was all the same - a herbal combination of dry seeds and shards of dusted crop conjured up in to an ever thicker tea or an even-fuller bowl of drum to make the heart grow fonder still. It worked. Fircle would cram his pipe in the morning, every morning, to get through the day and again in the evening to get through the night. He laid his head in the cloud or drank it down with a wash of lapsang to hide the golden scent and bleak out the distraughts of his most fragile thoughts.

50

It might have been the Valentine's Dance, the usual simple seductions played out across the western world of hormone charged teens trying to punch above their sea-level and find that spangled love-everlasting, their dreams pinned down to the final three minutes of slow dance-romance, tongues entwined and bodies pressed, such as the hopes held by Fircle, desperate still to rekindle the will of the way with Corina. The desperate hurt doing desperate things to hurt itself further, like sink-holed soul bonfires to clinker. Valentine's Day: the worst possible punishment of the lonely, inflicting a celebratory séance to contact the dead. He'd got himself dressed to the nines and tens and swashed his buckle as Bob would do.

He was waiting, with Limerick and Elle, getting drunk and gently stoned, as they sat in the upper hall. Jenniwren Joist was waiting too, waiting and wishing for the long-on linger with Dandy Djinn, that elegant swathe of indie-charm written through his innards like the words on a stick of rock. She had loved him from a distant swing, the swoon of never-too-soon candied-floss across the sighs of her eyes, the luckless longing to be but held in the arms of another's other embrace.

Fircle sat down by her side at the top of the stair and, since they'd already started when they'd sat in The Hangman getting half-cut, they carried on sharing their woes, passing the mystic fro and to as each of them slipped into the melancholy baby of their poverty-stricken dreams. As much as he tried, Fircle could offer her nothing by way of consolidated consolation, try as he might well have wanted: the final fracture had broken his will to be. Earlier in the evening, he'd been telling Pop all about his plans to meet up with Corina. Pop had tried in vain to warn him, to lay out a mat to break the fail of his fall that he could see so clearly was coming. But his son didn't listen. Instead, as soon as he got word of the whisper that Corina was there, he went bounding into the unlit hall to hold his meet and greet of sublime serenity and chapel. Lavender knew what awaited and had tried to catch his arm to forestall his long drop but he dashed past in all his dylanist desires, circa sixty-five: the black jeans, black turtle, black chelseas and wild woven hair, clattering down the stairs, knowing exactly how it feels but bringin' it all back home just the same to the game, to the run of the rails, and there and then she was, as he swung through the double doors, beauty framed in the light that came through from behind him, the guy in his dirt-bike boots, her arms up around his neck, and that same smile on her face that Fircle had once been given. And oh those adoring eyes he'd known himself just too few times. The world fell away from his feet and he fell through space and time towards and into the vacancy of the void. He wanted to disappear, to become as nothing and no one, invisible to every eye, the vanishing man, but there he stood, the fool, a jester in the court of the good saint's mocking laugh.

When he sat down again with Jen, there were tears already burning his eyes into dust. She signaled to Limerick who first passed a tinny and then two ready-rolled tokes to her. She opened the can and passed it to

Fircle, lighting then the first roll. She took a long, deep draw and they swapped. Then she told him the length and breadth of her own story from its dawn to its dusk, the limitations of lust and the longing and above all the purified poetry of the unrequited. Forever, in all its courtesies, he listened on in his own tears and Limerick kept them loaded, bombed on heavy, as a service to the foregone conclusions of their failures, to give them at least the hope of a hopeless redemption and Fircle threw himself in with full deliberance, knowing in that frame of time that only an oblivion can ever hold the cure.

51

The languid liquid of golden honey runs down the back of your princely eyes to succour any pole-ax protestations, to ague soft the limited visions of every elemental of your ne'er-do-well soul, the blank caucasian injuries of brattled mothers gosling the charms of their wearied lines and the dust between them gathers in measures stolen to the heights, the mule-kick, the sponsored dog, as derelict children bone-fancy and scupper their laments, beguile and bedeck their halls and judge not the ready-reckoning of soda'd simple cause and affectation, the Quincy's murmur, the open-toe of bull lee stubbing at the formulas of reason you reckon to have and have not the wherewithal or the where on earth the shattered glass has spoken in whispered voices of saintly women as oracle's standing in their delphi'd bare, of softest sole and gossamer skin, the drapes of finest silken sheen, the grapes of pristine piston posts all formed in rank and filed nails of sails and lone redemption the coxon waiving his handsome bride the boat beneath waves of water soluble insolvent banks beatific in casual graves their lonesome lions adrift in seaweed wells deep to the abyss in the garden, the octopuddle, the starman, the cray-fisher-king, the lobster potter throwing his gray clay at the walls of wedded blissed-out mansfield fire-placed on a pedestal to wonder be-wondered and thunders of tides washing away the lives of the loves of the livers shivered, shammed, shaken like boxglove marionettes dancing at the wail of the whale, the baleen, the bodene, the bow-line sang the melody at rats scurrying ants across the chest and tiny claws of tickled whiskers, clawed ringers digging at the face and fancied rants of formic acid dissolving the skull from the outside inside sideways and down the alley the ice wagon flewed an flewed it's rattled wheels adrift from the river arrived from the drift of the Rourke's, the roarks, the croaks the coax the drum-beat cum-beat battle forlorn forget and forgat the shit the shat the rainbow mat the cloak n dagger cat-call eyes akin to the ways of sin the wages of skin the peeling son burnt grin of the sun king son god standing at the guillo-gallow-tine swaggered on his stone scalp as the bucket beckons the knitters threaten jittered curmudgeon bludgeon the burrowing skull cats' fetid feasting burning down bootstrap apocalypse the bunting hunting its prey and tearing limb from the lamb of Marietoinette's pretty farm in the world, the weald, the wool-weld way of the samurai sword, to the seascape sewage of seward's brush with the law on the floor in the flim-flam flophouse destitute of reason summoning tangiered summits over boys in drag and stags in bragg and omniscient scientist grabbed the left-long lung screaming wisdom to the woman in the snugulent bar-stooled-booth of where be she oh the siren singing her smiled crescendo the yorkish yarm that's the level of a field of wakes an a season of snakes at crews controlled volume in the wish wife the eyes the voices the smiles skipping as stones on the Merrimack of sawyer samovars locked in ill-principle, the dancers gone beyone be-off; the disembodied body floating down caressed by silver maidens to love beloved the love the love the love and longing and to Capistrano swallowed in gentle kisses wishes and here be the joyful boyful adored in sleep to safely once again to sleep in seeping stands, and just just the rust of the busy remains to ghost its sleep to lull the by to sleep in deep beneath the beneath of beyond in wondrous butterfly kisses as lashes linger the longer the love, the love, the fool's gold rush.

52

Somewhere in the summertime a glorious house rolling down across the shield of the weald, doming up to meet the clearest stars. Limerick loading the pipe with drum and mystic, Lavender Backgammon swirling dervish curls and bottled-red by the side of cross-lain Fircle, mezcal-eyed to the skies, visioning the birth and floor of galaxies within galaxies, the dark between each empty space and its neighbour, the finest grains of phased light around each distant sun flickering like famed concertos, like ballerinas pirouette-startled amid the conch shell song of oblivious caribbeans of all eternity.

The lithium-swell of the tarantel beckoning waves of fingers, the pipe passing beyond the beyond to the lucid dreamboats, the lips alighting, the stunned petroleum flame in the mouth of mexican dreams kissed to the dreams of the brakeman's song, the galleyhand's swing and so to caress in the cornet's song the Boldenesque flurries o'er the scented muse, floral-dressed to the Indian-orbs gentle embrace.

He knew that she kissed him only because there was no Sophocles and never likely to be, that he was second-best at best, but none of that mattered in the moment, as she sat at his side, the both pie-eyed, dreams wide, as she raised herself to meet his kiss. And for one night he felt that such as this may last beyond the dawn, might even take them to the fall of the western world, when they'd even sit side by side and talk of things laid between the cracks in the pavement by gods of the random past

She kissed him and held him as if she knew his heart had dropped off the flat of the world and wanted to carry it in her purse to save it from the ocean's tears. She kissed him and held him as if the roadside picnic had eaten it's last and the road to wrack and to ruin had slept in the dust of time and all that could keep them had flown to the nest of the birds that inhabit the seven spheres of paradise. She kissed him and held him as if the flowers of the wilderness had grown into bloom and plume and the mysteries of the sea had settled to the sand to stand like the shadows of lost tomorrows. It was night, and in dreams do the sorrows find solace in tangled lips, fingers twined and foreheads resting against the other.

53

There is always a man you can see about a dog. There is always a doctor who doesn't know your name. There is always a door unlocked by the chemist at night. Mostly, you get smarties, fumbling in the dark, grabbing what falls. It's always tough on the tendons, difficult to get the timing right when flipping the coin in a blindfold ditch. Sweethearts were never so easy on the fly of the eye. You could fish for the ducks forever and never get that right.

The rolled gold of the joy of jones was the steadfast headfast blend that rose up high, riding on the rif from the berber mountains to the pashtoun fields. Jones came in with a kindly smile and an arm across the shoulders.

"Lemme help," said the jones, and Fircle took him up on the offer and the promise. It gave him a release that could be found in no other corner of the country. Not even the keeper of the kingdoms could ever or even guarantee that level of commitment: not the magic of mysticism, nor the latent leaning of lush, or even in the evening the unsubtle meltdown of his so many fiends. Not even the enfolding leandered meander of Lavender's arms took the world of the weight out of the unhappy hollow that he'd thrown himself in, although he'd have gladly thrown himself out of the window if she'd asked. She never did. She knew from the frame that he didn't play in her league, that he was strictly the bucket boy for the Sunday seniors. Besides, she was still so sweet on the philosophic Soph to turn even the blindest eye in Fircle's direction. So while the aisle of her smile and the flirts of her flowered skirts would be there while they sat snuggled on Limerick's mystic, he would always be found in the morning, fetal at the bottom of the stairs.

So Fircle and jones walked with a zombie as his dreams watched over them along Haitian shores of love's lost midnight, the monochromed mood-drop that plagued from a night in the prigged grip of spring to the closing time doors of India's summer.

HATEVILLE

54

Twa the gypsum kypsum, the Kip Gypsum? Maybe-baby it was in the socks of Soya Vaugham but surely not, she being that of a differentiated league of business from the merely of mortal. Either way, there she blows, the whale, the sail, the whited jack, the sack. The body, as if described in a novel, face down in the brook and bramble of imagination's woods, arms out-latched as if fallen from the cruciform with each and every clue going a-blessing for all to see.

And so they climbered and clambered over the scene of the crene, gather in their eyes for digestion all that could bear witness as words, just as the Good Doctor had taught them in his dissection of the cadaver of Jules Verne.

So could it be the Kyp Gypsum, desired yet now deceased? Fircle wanted to roll the page over to see but such was never the done thing to think, to read the last page, to forward-fast the frame, for as the kildare had spake:

"What use is the answer if you don't join the quest?"
So amongst the rummaging, oddly whispereding, they sought what gave the journey its meaning, its moaning, its groaning and jostled for the scent of a matchbook.

As some climbed to the hatch of the route back to their routine room, Fircle turned his ears back to the ripple of water and knew they were being read in return. Something beneath the science of the surface moved westwards and his eyes followed it, recognising the import.

Others had seen his face spewing knowledge and thoughts that couldn't be hid and soon cast about for evidence of criminality but none fell to their grasp. Fircle was being hollered home and left, returning to the paged box with their damp and the must and the water running down the insides of the walls as it rained. The Good Doctor was not there, so they sat and waited as if requiring permission to discurse. All wanted to know but none dared to share, case their words be used agin them in the court of lore that is standardised education.

55

If naught by nought else, the flight to Hateville got him away from Whorey Chorks and his endless supply train of afghan-berber from the west giving him the chance to eventually leave his jones behind in the company of better men than he. As much as he was going to struggle with changes that would be coming down the track like satan's train, he needed to start again. Start without the ragged cabbage baggage that draped from his limbs like a leper's rags. They say you never escape by running but he'd stayed too long and was drowning in the limits to the luckless sorrow of his addictions. And there was also the horror that he would be shacking with a family with small child in what had previous been a plod house, stuck at the arse of the end of town on the wrong side of the Scrag-of-Mutton Tavern. His curfew was at ten, but you didn't dare pass the Scrag any later than that anyway. He had little choice but to bundle his dreams into the body bag and leave them unto the cupboard's cadaver. He went to the cleaner's and left all but the lush in the gutter, hidden away in a six foot cell, curfewed to the ghost room while the rest of the world found their kith and their kin. Those first weeks were close to hell and would haunt at his days

If you had the choice before you knew there was the choice, you'd pick the old town, red brick style of Fleetfoot over its Hateville twin any day, even though it was a long old walk when the lights were low and the steak-stacking rare. It sprawled along a mile of the road that ran between the two towns, centering between The

Gnat's Chuff Inn and The Charlie's Aunt, after which it began to meld its way into a neighbouring city.

The Foot had the feel of a Laudenum microcosm with the rents and the rackets. Fleetfoot was where the immigrant communities had congregated - the Italians, the Jamaicans, the Portuguese and the Bengalis. It meant there was a wonder of good, cheap food from around the world to discover and the aromatic scent of spice was a life worth living. Those who had signed up to stake Combined Offal at the pyrotechnic tended to like that, especially the bit about it being cheap and the mix of exotic smells wafting out of the kitchens meant you could stroll the streets dragging on mystic without anyone noticing or giving a care. Those who could jumped in at the first chance they got. Fircle didn't get a chance. Before he knew what was happening, he found himself assigned to the grim reality of a single-cell-setting with a young family needing someone to help pay the mortgage.

56

Viola Shackleton was a stunningly beautiful spirit and Fircle was hit with the smit when first his eyes fell over the shock of her hair, each strand pulled to its outer-most stratum that the follicle could feel then frazzled to fold back and forth in every direction but north. As wild and volatile in every utterance as the devil could countenance or bear, she took them by the throat and tossed them down the stairs with abandoned gloss. Shaping the mother-of-pearl of the cut-throat like a rose petal swan, she took up the leap of laughter, shaved her scalp to the bone and stood with a raised fist.

As he folded his frame into one of the too-small chairs that each room was brimmed to colic with, how could he but help to notice the due similarity between himself and but one of her shorn-headed locks.

"Oh to be in Shackleton's arms," he bemoaned in his thoughts as he stared across the table like the wounded dog that he was.

"So, Lazlop. Your thoughts on the essentiality of syphilis in the development of philography?" It wasn't stated as a question. More like the final demands of a debt collector bent on suffering. The master and commander of all educators seemed to be born out of the innate ability to eye-spy those who had no fucking clue what they were doing there.

"I don't get it," Fircle confessed, "why it would need to be essential?"

"For pity's sake, boy, if it wasn't essential, why do you think we would spend long hours of our valued bothering to lecture the likes of you about it? The rest of you, which of you can deliver us from evil and forgive us our trespasses on this matter, since Lapslop clearly can't? Shackleton?"

The answer she gave was flawless and marble-sculpted, whatever it was, and whether she believed it or nay, it clearly showed that she had done the reverent reading. Others made liquid critiques that left important words hanging in the air like symptomatic flowers. While visible to all, Fircle tried to chalk them down to his lids before they vanished amid the pipe-smoke of futility.

This was possibly not the introduction he had hoped for. While he had read of the Taciturns of Diplodocus and was vaguely familial with the Epoxy-Resins of Fledermaus, he'd never actually read anything more thought provoking than the comics and his regular audience of similar backwater teens that could be fooled with a little lathe wordplay were now nowhere to be seen. Bereft of a backstop rounders, Fircle knew that he was in bad need of a book or two, although the will to actually open them and stare at the pages might come in handy as well.

"So, do you get it now?" the Rooster scorned across at him.

"It makes a bit more sense of scent, now."

"Oh, I'm sure it does." At which he was looking up to a far off corner of disbelief.

*   *   *

"Well, that went well for you," Amon pitied as he walked beside him. Up against the rack-spined Lazoon, even with the height of his quiffed quoff, the Oh Reilly looked like a small child. The mismatch in their washington heights and Amon's propensity for walking on his left meant that Lazoon had begun walking with a sideways piza.

"Who's the girl with the hair," he pleaded at that moment.

"Shackleton? That'll be Viola. She lives up on our floor," his diminutive friend told him, "She's..."

"Beer o'clock!"

He had been on the point of a scientific discovery of great import but Nicodemus had spotted them and knew of whence they were heading. The hidden mysteries of Viola, it seemed, would have to wait til later.

It was the Maus that had saved him from the pit in the arse of the pits, dragging him out by the lonesome leather of his bootstraps as he held on grim-like to a fear of all things by the quick of his broken fingers. She had lifted him out of the slow decline of terror at his existentials that would otherwise have consumed his gaping soul off the bridge on the long road to the north. She bundled him into a room in the borough of Fleetfoot. He had gone eventually under enemy fire, running from the dead-eyed stare of an eight-year-old boy, with a suitcase of second-hand books, a rucksack of rustic clothes and a typewriter. Maus had walked him out to the bus like a community care patient, rode with him on the freedom ride and introduced him to a ground-floor bed, an open house, a kitchen of motherly love and the blonded strawberry of Harvette, whose forebears had founded the medical mysteries of Harley Street in all its doctoral strategy. Cherry Coots would come in later to the folded aprons that Maus metaphorically wore and then there was finial Fynn, occupying the full main room of the house, out with the biddy-baxtered Nana and her steam-kinged beau. Within the space of just over the midnight of an hour, he had gone from the solitary cell of confinement to the gates of freedom and his mind quaked in the sheer blind terror of release. After a month or more of the sorrows of Sunday, he was able to smoke and drink and live as a human again.

Soya Vaugham wore a quiffed coiffure that even the presleytarians would have sacrificed the souls of their seventh-born sons for. With a solid jaw of deft defiance, she stood head and shoulders over all but a few, doc-shoed and strident, fierce as the devil himself and afraid of nothing and no one. She was everything most of them wanted to be, outspoken, with fist-raised intelligence beyond the mere paradiddle parroting of the taught. There wasn't a man jack among 'em that didn't look to her for the word - not the shaman-eamon of Amon, not the hippogriffed guitar of Nicodemus, nor the coolest strutting of the elegant Parker with his clean lines and charmed smile and certainly not the failed farce of Fircle. All heads would turn in the graves as she entered and when she smiled to your thinking, you knew you were safe from your own stupidity. That was the bean of Soya Vaugham, the maugham of all the summers to have set.

Fircle never saw her standing up with anyone and wasn't sure whether she was willfully alone in the world or kept her dreams well hid. Certainly she could have had any jill or jack of them had she wanted but he always thought that none of them was her match. She was central to their body in all ways, never far from the midst of being but seemed to be able to disappear at will to some other place or time and as a consequence she held a captured mystery that kept the world at large a-guessing. It may have been that she held an other in significance elsewhere but he never knew, as much as he may have wished to ask and such secret knowledge helped to hold her in the league's beyond. They knew that as much as she was their lead that love was out beyond even the tips of the fingers. For fear of falling backwards, all who would have wouldn't ask her. Soya was the terrifying emanance of womanhood, the beautied brain, styled in all such grace that none of them could gather the wits.

And so in heroic proportion Soya would stand amongst them, one of them, with all of them, a mother-warrior, their own boudiccea of the Hateville night. Always collected, never off her head nor lost in slurred and slurry. No one messed with Soya, or those who fell under her wing and those unwanted fools who tried to hide beneath soon found themselves aghast in the deserts of communion.

59

With the slush of the lush and the rake of the rum do the falling off the line and the launch run done and down. All thing do flash its mealy mouth and the cork of the coin do suck up the song.

"I'sh getinother," says eye an all bets nother. An there's never enough hands for the handle.

"Drink up, we'll get in another before they call time, same again?"

Same again.

Same again.

An the joy of the thin plastic beer glass that you carry it out as you please. But still there's only two hands and never enough time to keep drinking. Oh, to find such ways as to keep on drinking at the end of the night. So hold them tight like dreams and never let them drop. Let others go run for the last bus home; let others not stop in the rain to cover the last of the glass; let others not stagger in the streets and slump up the walls, or fall in the roof, or rant in the roost.

Oh for the lock-in

Oh for the late night offy

Oh for the all-night garage

Oh for the wit to have bought a half bottle of rum for the road while waiting for the bus. A tough call to make. Get the rum, miss the bus, arrive late like the no-mate you are and be stuck on the fringes, or be in on things from the get-go but not have the fall-back. But if you didn't need the fall-back, you would be in control, staying safely in your limits. Fircle had already long lost contact with limits or control. Once he started, he couldn't stop, couldn't refrain from the next and the next and the hopes of yet another before the final whistle blew.

60

But there in silence, everyone speaks in the end. You just need to wait out the waltz long enough and the weight of wax will break open the window, cracking it slowly at first as the pressure gains haste amongst the murmurs til finally bursting out and as the yammer came to a crescendo up spake The Doc with a shout:

"SO! WHAT HAVE WE LEARNED FROM OUR MEANDERS? SHOW ME!"

And they lead or he lead back to the body, each clutching their copy of *20 Pounding Leaks Beneath The Seats* for the moral support of a vernon's guidance. At which point they opened the mouthings and told all that was there to be telled:

"The body is face down."

"For why?"

"To hide the identity, so the reader doesn't know who."

"And be this a clue?"

"A clue in the hiding of the clue, we mustn't know because to know would be to reveal."

"Aha!"

"The matchbox! Firmly held and square in the knuckle..."

"And yet?"

"The arm is be-wrapped in bramble, so it must have been carefully placed."

Fircle huddled himself at the read of debate, afraid to unleash his own clue for fear of ridicule. But finally they had run down the list that the Good Doctor held in the glasp of his head and he had himself thrown but nought to the ring.

"There's the ripple..."

And it was out, at first flopping around like a landed fish dying in the sun, but there on the chopping board it lay, and then they began to wonder, allowed - could the killer be held in the brook itself, breathing, perchance, through the hollowed-out reed of redemption.

61

The House of Heaven was well-placed in the centre of Fleetfoot. With an undertakers, church and cemetery at the end of the road, it sat within striking of the main route between Hateville and Ste. Sebastién, the latter an easy stroll, the other a five mile hike or a hitch. Maus also had the battle tank that they only used to go on the run for the big shop, due to its high consumption of the environment.

Five of them eventually shared a building that any other landlord would have crammed in double that. As a consequence, their house was seen as high luxury, despite the collapsible ceilings and dangerous tiling. Whereas most students lived in houses with doubled-up rooms or bunks with galley kitchens as their only shared space, they each had their own privacy with a kitchen-lounge big enough to hold a party and one which, despite the fungus growing on the walls in one, boasted two bathrooms. No one they knew had seen such levels of splendour and refinement. And no one they knew paid so little in rent.

The icing on the cake, however, was the walking wonder that was the motherly Maus. Not that she forever changed their pads and wiped their butts but Maus, like all mothers, was organised in a way that made falling out of bed in the morning a joy and she could be relied upon to teach you to tie your own bootlaces to the wall. Even the finicky Fynn with his aged stance of the long-standing studier discovered a whole new world of personal hygiene from the examples set by this master magician of the homely hearth.

"Ee, Firky, will you do me the washing up," she'd call in her cheery northern brogue, straight out of the western hills of Maudlin, "an' I'll fix us some tea if you do?" and with an offer like that of imminent egg-fried rice, who could but argue the odds.

Such were the comforts that others could only dream of in their wildest, someone to lead them from the cloisted foisted on the unwanting world and into the age of adults, able to cook and clean and use the launderette without fear of burning the residue. It was Maus that showed them how to bake like alaskans and melba the peaches, while others made do with pots of noodle nausea. Sharing a Haus with the Maus made anyone the luckiest dog in the pound.

62

Wilbur Biddy was Nana's little brother and he entered the world like a whirlwind. He would eat the house and the home as well but otherwise lived on a diet of European beers and mystic. He'd been living in Germany for longer than anyone could fathom but had grown up on a Wiltshire farm when milk was still delivered in the churn on a horse-drawn buggy. In years as few as Fircle's, he had circum-navigated the world, beaten out the avalanched roofs of expensive cars and bought himself a camper van that became his home and place of refuge from the torment of the world's petty vices. That was all the way until he met Harvette.

He bounded in with Nana Biddy one mid-March morning and then never seemed to leave. They'd come to see Fynn, or at least Nana had, and while she stood fixing Fircle's attention as the dream-like elder, Wilbur wound his way to the kitchen and proceed to fix himself some food.

"Ah'm so sorry," he laughed, "but ah'm blooming famished."

He explained that he'd been driving first east then west and then back east again chasing papers for his sister that had gone for a walk somewhere between the two. Fynn, it seemed, was a likely provider of carbon copies, although he was out on the milk run, which might take anything from a minute to a millennium, although given that it was Maus that had sent him on his fetch-errand, it was likely to be the former, due to her perfected training.

As they were waiting for Fynn to make his reappearance, Harvette wafted in as she always did, like a dandelion seed blowing by on the wind, her tumbles of hair pre-raphaeliting over her shoulders, and with his mouth still biting into his multi-storey sandwich, Wilbur was smitten, bitten by the bug that beats in all of us. From that point on, he and Harvette were an inseparable feature of the household, in the only room that was shared by two, it also being the smallest room in the building.

It was Wilbur that had given him the name Firky, the name that everyone eventually took to calling him. It turned that, after years of calling him this, Wilbur wasn't just rolling out a new nickname but genuinely thought that was what he was called. It seemed to him to be just as good as any other moniker and he just followed what he'd heard and everyone, Fircle included, went along for the ride.

This was nothing new in the roll of time. He'd been called many things over the years and tended to respond to most, whether out of recognition or desperation. A name was just another way of not being able to hide from the world when he was out in it. With a name, you couldn't go curl in the corners of existence for the people still found you and called you back to their world. There were times when the beauty of no-self seemed such a tide of bliss: to be naught but nothing, not need to hide behind the bottle but just to disappear into the eco-system of the empty void. To be but nowhere. Nihil.

63

As an act of his drunken generosity, Fircle was prone to drinking beyond both his own capacity to stand and his ability to make it as far as the last bus to get back to the house in Fleetfoot. What this meant was that he became a regular body dumped on the various floors and left to snore through til the dawn. Amon was the usual victim, even despite his attempts to maintain a level-bedded relationship with the force of nature that was Velma Bookshelf - yet another who could read the world beyond Fircle's remedial eyesight. Although Guernsey Puck would become similarly afflicted and suffer the slinks and harrows of outrageous gluttony. Gradually, he became a featured figure in the nightmares of those who cooked late or woke early, appearing in kitchens in the midnight hours roaring with joys or be-staggering the halls at the break of day, sweating out the alcohol through the clothes he'd slept in, with the bloodshot eyes of a demoned devil-dog. Whichever end of the night they found their encounter, he was an ominous sight to behold and he put the fear into many an unwary soul.

On a rare occasion, he walked up to the cardboard portacabins that passed as student accommodation, one time dragging Puck behind him wrapped in the net of a football goal and, in a final bout of glory, with the great mystery of his year that had been the heart skipping wonder that was Viola Shackleton. Every other time, she had seemed to be in transit to somewhere other, somewhere else, stopping for a short while, but always so very short, never pausing for long as if there was always so much more that needed to be done - another meeting to attend, another lecture, a book to be read, a tale to be told, another voice to be heard calling from the wilderness of thought. However often he sat with her to share a cigarette, they would soon be off again until their lives could once again intersect. They would talk of feminist theory or the value of a good set of shears for a closer crop. As friends they were intermittent, it sometimes being a week or more before their paths would ever cross. Even then, as they would smile to each other and pause as long-lost acquaintances, it would so often only to be to greet and farewell before each made their storm-wrought way to a different corner of the world.

But this night had turned into that rare-as-hens'-teeth moment when Viola had entered the bar at the same time as Fircle and both had an open evening ahead. They'd been sat with the charm of Parker, with Amon, with Guernsey Puck, roaring with laughter until the glorious quiff of the former was forced to separate Puck from the channel of his islands and they just left as the Vee of Velma danced in to pin-down the whereabouts of Amon. These four had drunk their way through the rest of the night, with others drifting through and beyond. Maus had come over around eleven to see if Fircle was going for the last bus but his thirst, as always, was in no mood now to stop and both Amon and Viola were wishing him to stay for a little longer. Finally, after a year of chasing her, only to find himself chasing his own tail, he had sat his set with her for longer than the curt at-best half-hour and they were at last coming to know each other as if of old.

The four hung around til midnight, finishing their drinks and starting others until time was finally called, and as Amon strolled off arm-in-arm with Velma, Fircle figured that, if nothing else, he should walk Viola back through the dark to finish the closeness of their conversation. But once there, she offered him a coffee and they carried on talking in the communal kitchen, on and on through the hours, occasionally holding hands across the table in shared spirit. Around three or four in the morning she said:

"I really need to get some sleep. But... I can't have you stay over. I... I know how you feel... about me... and, I really do like you but... I'm with someone else."

"That's okay," he said as gallantly as he could muster with all his walls once again crashing down, "I figured you probably were. You're too nice a person not to be."
He may well have sounded like he was fighting to hold back a primordial wail of degenerate despair but in his own mind he was the Buddha, calmly explaining the middle way to a disciple.

"Do you want to have another coffee with me before you go?"

"Nah, I'm okay. Besides, we'll end up talking for even longer and you'll never get any sleep. And I've drunk so much coffee in the last couple of hours I'll be awake for days meself."

"It's cold out tonight," she told him, but he'd been so lost in talking that he hadn't noticed the state of the weather outside. He stood and put his jacket on.

"It's fine. It's only a short walk."

"Let me... let me get you a jumper, so you don't catch cold." Viola dashed out of the kitchen and ran to her room, coming back almost immediately.

"Please take this. Please. I don't want you to get cold. Please wear it. For me."

Fircle gave her what he thought was a winning smile but which may have come across as a feral grimace and took off his jacket again.

"Okay, for you. But I don't want you thinking that I accept warm clothes from just anyone on a cold night. I'm not that kinda guy."

She laughed. The jumper smelt so closely of Viola, her scent, her skin.

"Thank you," he said finally, reaching out a hand to hers and squeezing it gently, "you're very kind... and a very beautiful person." Viola may have blushed but he was already heading out the door.

The skeen of the day began at the half of seven, standing out in the morning light awaiting the ceremonial unlocking of the minibus. Most of them were fellow check-ins from the Pyrotechnic. All but Fircle were fresh blood, barely off the teat, thrown into the world of work too soon for the good of themselves or the world itself.

"All in," said the Lard, sliding back the side door before opening up the front for the groupies who were blessed to sit up front where they could at least wind down a window on the world as they went by. The Lard liked the young girls to sit up front with him where he could assume the role of lothario. They were not long out of their pinnies. Not yet twenty. Twenty had passed Lard by. As had thirty. He was now renting a room at his mother's, earning his meagre means driving people to & fro the various factories, six til nine in the morning, four til seven as the sun set down, five days a week and overtime at the weekends. But as shit as it was as a way to earn a crust, it was still better than succumbing to the factory work itself.

Maus and Harvette were themselves locked in the warm embrace of the Slab-o-Cheese, where they skimmed the mould off the slabs before fine-quartering them for retail, a skill that required the garroting of a foot-long block of reconstituted cheddar into roughly equal quarters with a metal wire and vacuum-sealing it before the mould could crawl back up off the floor to take a second hold. It required elements of precision for which Fircle's fatted fingers were supremely unsuited. That and his inability to withstand the morbid fascination of watching that thin green crust reform itself into a living mass on the floor and begin to work its way closer to satisfy its hunger.

There was also the problem of footwear as Fircle's over-enthusiastic feet put him at odds with the assorted sizes of safety boot available to him at The Slab, and 'tho the grafter worked tirelessly throughout the shift to keep the green plague at bay, there were times when the skimmers had to resort to blasting their boots with the steam-hose to keep the scum down. Without boots, he wouldn't have survived a day.

It had occurred, the previous summer, that mid-grift the grafter had suffered a massive seizure, brought on by a double-shift exposure to mould spores. He had shoved the scraper the length of the floor when it happened and as a consequence he was out of sight of those working on the line. So no one noticed him keel in the corner, a dead man, not having managed to make the mark of the final shunt of the seething mass to the sewer hole.

He had been the first to go, although technically speaking he had already gone but once devoured down to the bone, the falling skeins reformed once more and a quiet lady long-since beyond the span of her commercially valued days became the second - Avril Scorecard. It crept from behind, over the top of her work boots, up her trousered legs, the white coat, within the sleeves, over her face and leaving the hair-cover-hat untouched. If it hadn't been for the change of shift at the end of the day, the mould would have moved up the line, taking each in turn and consumed them all, one by one.

Avril was no doubt still sentient as they began to peel away the coating of green, but it was already embedded into the fabric of her being by the same tenderous fibres that it attached itself to cheese. To use the steam-hose would have left what was left of her with third degree burns and while her fingernails were best, exposing the fleshless hands was inadvisable. So they borrowed a consignment of cheap window squeegees from a garage down the road and began the delicate act of removal.

Anyone who has ever entertained the vain quest of removing ice from a winter windscreen with a credit card will know why it was that by the time they had cleared her mouth and nose, Mrs Scorecard had departed to that great cheese factory in the sky.

Fircle was, therefore, destined not for the Slab-o-Cheese but for the equally repellent Bone Chicken Arcade.

65

Beefchicken was the speciality of the Bone Chicken Arcade. It was a combination of processed chicken-grind and the finest cattle cast-offs that money could buy in profitable bulk. If you took these together and added a plug of prime reconstituted fat, you could turn out some of the greatest culinary wonders that the microwaveable ready meal could conjure south of the gates of Westward Ho! All you needed was a drone of bodies to slice and slam the ingredients together and the front to sell it as food.

The day started at 8 with a tea-break. Nothing could be packaged until whatever needed cooking in the kitchen had been sufficiently boiled into submission, so the kitchen boys had already been in since six. With four deep vats sitting over gas pipes that stuck up out of the floor, two for the carbs and two for the sauces, there were two teams, one for each side of the kitchen.

The carbs churned out either rice or spaghetti. For the sauces, it was either gravy or sweet & sour - there was no bolognaise sauce to go with the pasta, that was just the cheapest way they'd found of creating something that looked like noodles. The only other job the kitchen boys had was to roll out a variety of semi-frozen vegetables from the freezer, crack open the sacks and empty them into a giant wheeled colander bath and roll these out to the lines where some muppet shovelled it all out into trays for the women to weigh and load. Most days, that muppet was Fircle.

It was only ever women who worked the line. Old, young and everything between; light-skinned, olive-skinned; and any shade of black or brown you could mix; but always it was women. Men were restricted to anything truly grim. The grimmer, the better. If it involved heat, pain, blades, flames, sweat and tears or tyranny then it was obviously a job for men. Fircle became well-acquainted with all of them.

66

It was going to be a week of gravy. A week of gravy meant a week in the chiller. Door shut. 1°c. No contact with the outside world. No clock. No sound but the steady whirr of the slicer.

He got to work straight away. No one could work until the meat was cut, so while everyone else was getting some breakfast, he prepped the machine.

"Sliced or diced?"

Sliced was beef, gravy, peas carrots. Diced was beef, rice, gravy, peas, no carrots. He set the machine and pulled in the first trolley - a set of four, eight-foot long shelves on wheels that were stacked high with thigh-sized lumps of processed beef loosely wrapped in plastic sheets to keep the flies off while it had been standing outside. There were four trolleys waiting. It would be a long, grim, bloody morning.

You roll the slab of meat into a slot. If it's too thick to go and it's defrosted enough, you hack some off to make it fit. Otherwise, you beat it down with a mallet, hammering it home, the slot being only five inches wide and the slabs always being wider. Sometimes, the lumps were so large that you have to chop them down to size with the guillotine, but that slows everything down. The slower you go, the slower the lines go and the more everyone complains.

So you slammed in the beef slabs, pressed the green button, grabbed for another slab, listened for a jam, listened for the bolt to withdraw and the tone of the spinning blade to change, opened the safety guard, slammed in the slab, pressed the green button.

You took the smaller slabs first because cutting the big ones down to size was harder when they were still fresh from the freezer, only having been out for maybe half an hour. That early, they were like solid bricks and chopping them down to fit the machine was cold, hard labour.

In twenty minutes, you could fill a bath tub and you'd be wheeling it out as the tea-break was finishing. They could start, but you'd be back in the chiller then for the rest of the day. Prep the slab. Load the slab. Green button. Prep the slab. Load. Green. Prep. Load. Green. Fill the bath, open the door, shunt out the bath. Shut the door. New bath. Prep the slab. Load. Green. Prep. Load. Green. Prep. Load. Green. Open. Shunt. Close. Bath. Prep. Load. And you just keep going til the trolley is empty. Then you start on the next one.

As the day rolls on, the slabs defrost and it gets a lot easier to squeeze them into the slot and any cutting down to size is easier. But the plastic sheeting fills with blood, it covers your hands, sprays up as you slam the slab in the slot and stains your skin with the globs of fat clinging to the hairs on your bare arms.

By the fourth trolley, the chiller room had become like an abattoir and he had to stop. Hose out the machine to get as much of the fat, blood and scrag on to the floor. Bin the plastic, thereby covering your arms in more blood, then squeegee the floor to get as much of the waste, the blood, the fat, the scraggy grinds of death over to the sewer grating. Then lift the grating and squeegee it all in. Manna from heaven for any rats. He shut the grating and turned to trolley number four. Everyone else went to lunch and any baths still holding beef were left for him outside the chiller. He rolled them in, filled two more baths and left them all ready to be collected, then went to the washroom.

In the mirror, he could see the reason no one came to check on him. His overalls, hygiene hat, plastic apron and boots were something out of a horror film. His face was covered in splatters of blood and specks of fat, with the skin of his arms and hands stained a rancid reddish brown. He washed off the worst of it, hung up his apron and hat and went to the canteen. There was a plate of scrambled egg on toast waiting for him and Sylvia poured him a fresh mug of tea.

"Cold?" she asked.

"Frozen," he replied.

"Sit yourself down, love. I'll bring you another in a mo."

Within a few minutes of sitting down, everyone else had returned to work and Fircle was left on his own. Sylvia would bring him a second mug of tea and then get on with clearing the canteen. When he'd finished, Fircle put his apron and hat back on, headed to the chiller and the four new trolleys that were waiting for him.

67

"Wha'd'ya want, Trog?" shouted the Deacon, without missing a beat of the stirring paddle.

Fircle looked over his shoulder to the door and just caught the disappearing back of Annie as she headed back to the line. Troglodyte Annie got her name for the fact that her big sister was a supervisor who none of the kitchen boys liked. Even her brother who worked the stores and sometimes helped with the sauces called her Trog, although never to her face. None of them called her by her rightful name but that was because none of them ever spoke to her, except to shout abuse. Very few people did seem to talk to her, except some of the older ladies who mothered her like old barren hens.

"Piss Off!" the Deacon shouted after her over the top of the boiling water and the flames, "think the troglodyte fancies you 'arry," he nodded towards Fircle, "I tell ya, she better not bloody fancy me."

"Who fancies who?" Irish asked as he wheeled an empty tub into place.

"Trog fancies 'arry," Deacon confirmed and he threw his paddle across the room at Killjoy, "Oi! Killer, Trog fancies 'arry."

Irish was gone in laughter. Killjoy, though smiling, was retrieving Deacon's paddle from under the sauce vat before the flames caught.

"Give over," complained Fircle, but it was too little, too late. Irish had gone out with the bath of fresh spaghetti and even the sound of water flushing out of the vat couldn't drown out the sound of his voice:

"Factory announcement! Factory announcement! Troglodyte Annie fancies Harry Half-a-head!"

After a couple of circuits, he came back in, rubbing his hands with glee.

"You utter, utter bastard."

"So I am, Harry, so I am. Think I'll be taking my lunch with you today my son. Okay with you, boss?"

"Oh, I think it's an early lunch all round," the Deacon confirmed. Fircle's heart sank.

He was only saved from total humiliation by the line that Annie was on being held back to finish prepping the last of an order. But that didn't stop Irish from relishing the moment's long half-hour of ridicule, ensuring every biddy o' the bus knew his business. The older ladies went into mother-hen mode and became matchmakers while the young girls went into a wild flap. From there on in, he got no rest and it was all he could do to keep from crying.

68

Even in the canteen, she didn't seem to be part of the clique of local teen girls that always sat together. She was with them but never seemed part of their sect, which made it just a little strange that Fircle had found himself standing by the clock-stump at half-nine on a Saturday morning waiting for her to turn up. Good god, it was a Saturday morning! Fircle hadn't seen one of them in months. His usual Friday night routine precluded such things as it generally involved getting so drunk that he could forget that work was waiting again on the Monday and then trying his damnedest to retain that state for the next two days.

"H-hun," she sort of snort-giggled, twisting the heels of her white court shoes from side-to-side next to him. He half-jumped and she made the same nasal chuckle again. He sagged against the monument, looking down at her well-scrubbed, rosy-cheeked face. Out of her work clothes, she looked so incredibly young. He tried to figure out if she was still smiling, if she was pleased to see him. Annie had one of those faces where it was always hard to tell. What didn't help was that his hangover was still rotten. He was sweating red wine and had been drinking the dregs since waking up in an attempt to cut the mustard.

Yet there they were - Fircle, Annie, her friend from the factory whose name he'd never bothered to learn and the girl's boyfriend, not a day over fifteen, who was bobbing excitedly in tow. At nineteen, he was at least fourteen dog years older than any of them but where they'd only just come out of their school uniforms, he had passed out in ditches, woken up in derelict houses and seen a lifetime of his own horrors that was beyond their ken. It would be their only date. Whatever Annie had been expecting, it wasn't a hung-over, half-drunk who kept trying to lead them into the nearest pub. Whatever world it was that Fircle had come from, she didn't want any part of it. A fortnight later, he was back at the Pyrotechnic.

69

Coming from the outside by road, you hit the Northern Way which rings the city into its own fixed plague zone, but further out you hit the motorway and as everyone knew, everything within the motorway's circuit was also Laudenum, whether the residents liked it or not. But Fircle always went in by train, and then you by-passed the Northern Way and hit the Severed Head Station, the point from which all rails ran to the true north. And from there he could double back on himself and into The Clampdown, the cultural centre of Laudenum north of the Thames and also his favourite haunt for records, books, sitting on the kerbside, getting drunk and watching the beautiful people come and go.

Most weekends, Fircle had been finding himself there. At the time, the railways refrained from employing anyone to actually check your ticket, so if you couldn't afford to pay you just travelled for free. It meant he could head down to Candlewick to see his brother, or head right through to see the folks, or head up to The Clampdown without paying a penny.

He would flick through the Dizzy Gillespies, check out the beatnik books or sit on the street with a bottle of thunderbird and watch as the sun fell down behind the buildings, blood orange in the skies over Laudenum and such beauty as there never was on the earth before that moment. On a good evening, you could witness the way the world will end as night fell and the city took on its electric glow. On a better one, beneath slow and heavy rain, a screw-top bottle in a paper bag, and hugging the wall beneath the last remaining awning, it was possible to know the lonely sorrow of all existence, that every love is lost like the rivers running waste down through the gutters. Track out of time in The Clampdown, the clam town, wine bottle in hand like the gland and barely able to stand. There in the falling rain, the palling plain of the drunken drain. Such were the nights he loved the most, when he could stay there til the evening's final sad goodbye to the day. Such nights don't last forever; the rain will stop, the awnings will close along with the shops beneath them and with no one else to turn to, the last train beckons to be held.

70

While Fircle had gone for a standard fender acoustic, following where he could afford his folksome idols, the weapon of choice for most was the slimline semi with the f-holes. Some, of course, would cling to those basic variations on the strat but the predominance of style in the age of jangly-pop had created a host of heroes who went in for a hollow-body model. Nicodemus was one. Guernsey Puck was another. Both of them nifty-fingered.

And while there were more polished and refined sounds around the vicinity, most were stuck in the realm of the sultans of the virginia plains. The music they played was as staid as the grave, complete with the solo'd facial contortions accompanied by endless, weary guitar. If you wanted to dance, if you wanted your wig to flip, and if your pockets were devoid of all but buttons and bows, then you put in a call to Nicodemus and the Turk McGurks.

They would jangle and rangle through wild sounds like cowboys clinging on at the rodeo, forever almost falling, failing but always fiercely defiant of collapse: they rocked your jelly and they rolled your soul. A solid beat, a thumping bass, dual guitars and Nico wailing across the top, they could raise your stomp and graze your groove from dusk til dawn, barely stopping to drink or draw breath.

Their sets would start hard, roll mellow and peak every three or four songs, usually leading to a pitch invasion by their adorings, followed by a pause to refill, clear the stage and start again. The dancefloor never stopped pounding, and no one sat to rest or recover. The Turk McGurks were the rock to the roll, the shock to the stroll, the mamba biting the samba and the funk in the pockets of punk. The steam would rise as if a hundred writhing shaman were reading the rites, conjuring Robert Johnson's spirit to rise, the ground pooling dripping sweat to feed the snake of the world amid the holy screams of unknown joy, penultimating into a stage-diving, monkey-driving, stepping stone to a stop. Halting as if waking in hell, staggering back down, about to find a seat, and the encore would hit, the ten-minute crackle and flame of the voiceless mystery that was the *Rancid Jam*, a rollicking thrash over two chords that no one ever wanted to end, and it only did when Bradley, the exhausted drummer, called time, gentlemen, please.

71

He woke with the cold chapping at his knees and knuckles. Rolling the rock sideways, eyes a-closed and toes adrift, he could feel the spread of damp along the length of his spine and water falling lightly on his face. He now knew where he was and it definitely wasn't home. With the road between Hateville and Fleetfoot being just five straight miles, it was an easy hike in the light of day, and not so bad at the end of a night out after the last bus had long since gone its way. But Fircle had been so drunk he could once again seldom stand, so drunk he hardly knew who he was, so drunk his shame had left his bones to ruin its testiculated scream across the octave. Again. So he had laid himself down in a ditch to sleep it off beneath the stars that van gogh swirled in motion sickness movements up above.

He'd been in the bar at five and didn't stop drinking until they'd pushed him out the door. With no Amon to abuse the hospitality of, the next he knew, he was waking up in the rain in a roadside drainage ditch as the dawn was just beginning to crack the darkness.

Headlights tore through the guts of the morning, hit his eyes and split his head wide open with the cleaver of a Glasgow butcher. Nausea crept up with the subtlety of a dum-dum bullet and he was forced down on to the grassy bank, hunched over with his feet in the mud and his head up his arse. As the downpour continued, the bottom of the ditch was becoming a stream and the water was filling into his boots. He wanted to lift his feet out of the mire but didn't have the wits to do so. Passing cars were beginning to notice him, some slowing to look at the wreck in the rain of the dawn as they passed.

Fircle found his keys in his overcoat pocket and was at least assured that when he finally made it back he could get in the door. All he needed to do now was make it another three miles to get home.

72

His jones had returned of old, through force and fiend and the fact of the hole in the sole of his substance. He could find no way out to set himself free from the constant need to hide himself behind the drapes with the lone street lamp creeping its fingers through the gaps. Long distance or short, his head wouldn't cope with the chaos that rattled around inside. The doctor had said to quit drinking but only the lush made sure of the sense of every wakeful walk out the door: only by drinking and smoking all of Maus' cigarettes could he face the death of the day or the birth of the cosmos; only by falling himself beneath the wagon's wheels did the lack of his face in the mirror not threaten to shatter its grip; only by breaking the bottle on his skull could he hope to fill it with the tears from his eyes. He drank constant, no longer able to make the break between any of the worlds into which he had fallen, and only by stepping back into the darkness that he'd once cleansed from his bones could he ever hope to separate the sorrows.

Longfellow had been junked into jail, caught behind the wheel of a sulphate-stacked motor; Bullett had been cast from the guild for peddle; and Chorks had been chalked up to the gravestone, a victim of his very own dealings. And under a different doctoral regime, no one was falling for the lay of the lie. The peppered corns became harder to find, higher in price, while the seeds and their shells and the dusted chaff that he brewed in a china sea had doubled the cost and trebled the trick. All the world and all its wonders could now be forgot and forgiven, left to run the course of time without the need for Fircle's participation. Suitably steeped in the joy of his jones, he would sit at his desk in front of his typewriter, his ghost-friend stood behind in the guise of lost loves gone to the winds, massaging his tired, steinbeck shoulders to hemingway him into an act of inspiration never to come. There was nothing and he was one with it, himself a void of empty words and all the strains of being sane dropping like leaves in autumn. He lived by the lush, the china tea, the mystic and the new-found fiend, no more of a man, a receptacle for the nothingness of being, desperate to be saved by someone – no matter the circumstance or the love laid out as an offering – but incapable of saving himself.

73

In the oubliette of existence, parallels of chance beckon with a reckoning hand and the ghost of Carroll's lewis-gun stagger through the dreamlike butter thru a knife & crackle the seam, as if in despairing retirement where only the old survive their youths. Which is why they founded themself in the odd-shaped-room, cubic an' angled to emphasize the slide into derogation. Twas a jumble of bit-parts, like a treasure-hunt in a junk-shop of hyphenations.

So they rifle thru the trifle, playing as only adults do, imitating the precision of a child's logic, our foots all cakey with the flakery of the swamp-bed of the brook and having found the water-snake-charm knew no longer now what they may have made and found to be known and unknown.

"Bejiggered be I," quoth Amon Oh Reilly as he truffled among the scuffle of vinyl, seeing what would be worthy of filch and formentation. And so leaving aside the lamentation and the weep 'n' wail of evidence gathering they flocked their sheep's as a murder of crow to caw upon the quality of the body's collection, the each of teach of leaving with more than they can but leaving perhaps the portrait of Aunty Joyce in spectacles and fedora that hangst from an awkward wall to access, stompy-footed bootstraps left in the gentle remarks to the scene's reader. And then and then and then they appeared in the next visualisation of investigation, looking as looking does over the matter of their findings to see what it was they knew and no nothing.

"So what have we established of the baredom of the factuality?" The professor professed, and they sagely nod as nodding does, each one eyeing the eye of the other, awaiting a sacrificial lambkin to appear before and throw them own on to the oven of ideas. Symposing thoughts on the table, they edge the edging of dog-eared pages, notebooks and notarisms.

"Possibly," Fircle began, hesitant in the desire to sagistically state a stable case for the route, "we are looking at a staged event."

"Staged? Staged??? But of course it is staged, boy, as all such writing is writhed in stages by an author's own stagger," he mocked, his grey-beard chest-trembling with each chuckle of power wrought against the enemy.

"Perhaps," Soya leaned in, herself holding the words in her mouth as if waiting for concepts to form themselves into a fruit, "what Firky was trying to express is that the scene of the shine of the crime, as staged by the murderer, was itself a staging, so that the author was 'creating' something which was itself a creation of somebody else..?"

The professor studied her face in the silence, looking perhaps at the speed limit of her perfect quiff which the cogitations ground to their coffee. He looked then to Fircle who sank and stank in skank:

"So you're saying the author of this killing is a plagiarist?" he accused, and his unhappiness was as clear as the ringing of the bells on a Sunday. Fircle took the lifeline that Soya had thrown:

"Not plagiarism, as such, professor but..." he frantically longed for a word.

"Something more intangible?" Soya offered.

"That's the word! Intangible. As if, in staging the scene of the crime, the author has himself become the unwitting... no, that's not quite right, unwitting suggests a culpable lack of wherewithal wits, the victim of a thread of memory that has burrowed into the Freudian slip."

"Yes..?"

There hung in the air the urge for further clarification, the professor, with all in tow, becoming increasingly invested in the fabrication that Soya and Fircle had brokered. But the effort of toil was telling its toll. Young Amon stepped into his breeks.

"So, without being aware, openly and actively, the author's murderer has authored a scene that owes a tribal allegiance to the craven hand of another, not in the wistful prettiness of the copycat killer, seeking dim circumstance of a greater approval, but in the wealth of knowledge that accumulates the diligent study, a wealth of understanding that seeps into the very fabric of one's being."

Amon was adept in the arts of bullshit and acting in the puckish plausibility and the professor was seemingly satisfied with the patting of ego that he had been given. He nodded with sage and onion stuffing at the definite plausibility that had fallen open in its casket to be banked into a forthcoming book-deal on the vernish varnish of that year's underwhelming output.

74

The early mourning grime of misted dirt on the windows broke through just enough light with the chill of the morning to tear through the cut of the comatose and make him open his eyes to the crack of the day's babylon. Nausea of a stomach emptied of everything but the stain of whisky and wine swam up him out of his heels. His head's dehydration soaked down to his dry throat. His lungs demanded a cigarette but his body heaved in response. He was cold to the bone and tried to sit so he could wrap his coat a little tighter across his chest. And he found then that his shoes and socks had both gone.

Wherever he was, it had to be somewhere near The Clampdown. He'd been there Friday afternoon, looking for Dizzy Gillespie records, when he stopped to get some red wine to wash down the freshly-baked bread he was eating. He'd been sat outside the Compendium of Books with both feet in the gutter, watching the end of the day drift on without him, listening to the shutters start to fall and the crowds making their ways towards the Dingle Dell, the Legs of Devon or The Royal. He'd been talking to the street people that congregated there and when they'd all been thrown out of The Royal as soon as they'd put a foot in the door, he'd bought thunderbird and a bottle of bells which they'd sat drinking through til... til when..? Til dawn's early light. So they'd finished it and what?

Fircle slumped along the hallway to the front door with its broken-out lock where Big Bloke had kicked it open. They'd been laughing about it when he did it, and it had been dark. Skinny Pete had been hanging on the lamppost. Was that a different day? One scene of darkness and another of light fled through the cells of memory that remained on board for the bargain.

Stepping out into the haunt of the day, he felt the full weight of the morning's justice hit him on the back of the head with a cosh and he sank down to the floor. As he sat amongst the heaps of rubbish that accumulate around derelict and boarded up buildings, his bare feet sitting in what may well have been his own vomit, Fircle realised that yet again he didn't have the wits to know his own name, let alone where or when he was or what day it might be. Certainly, on Saturday morning, he'd still been in the top end of The Clampdown. Except somewhere in between then and now he'd carried on drinking and then woken up cold as death on bare floorboards without his shoes. He checked his pockets. And without his travel card. Or his bank card. Or any money. He could still feel the pressure of his door-key through his jeans pocket, which was at least one saving grace. But his cigarettes had all been smoked and so had his pipe with the secret pouch of fool's gold chaff that he kept on hand for just such an emergency. This lack of resources made him shiver as the symptoms of his existence kicked in.

A big red bus rolled by, which at least meant he knew what message he was in. It should also mean there'd be a bus stop close at hand so he could figure out what end of Laudenum he found himself hung-over in.

75

Among the morning's commuters, the young man cut a strange and, to some, alarming figure. Red-eyes and sickly pale, his retro raincoat hung like a rag from his shoulders, filthy-dirty down the length of one side and creased all over like an old man's face. Standing, barefoot, beneath the shelter, there was a good metre's distance between him and anyone else in any direction. Whether it was fear of the unknown or some distasteful odour that kept them away was unclear for none said a word and they could easily be turning their noses up at his appearance as much as the smell. For his part the man was still unable to distinguish the taste of vomit still in his mouth and nose from anything else around him.

Fircle stood back and let everyone else on first and when they had boarded he stood in the doorway.

"Do you go to Severed Head Station?"

"I do."

"Can I cadge a lift there?"

"One twenty."

"Me money's gone and me shoes've been nicked," to which he raised a foot as show-and-tell.

"Jesus," the driver laughed to himself, "get on mate. Looks like you might've made a weekend of it."

Fircle hauled himself aboard.

"I'm not sure. What day is it?"

"To you, mate, it's Monday. All day."

"Monday? Oh god."

"Sounds like you lost more than your shoes."

"Me shoes. Me money. Me wallet."

"Was it worth it?"

"Is it ever?"

At which point Fircle slumped into a seat and those close by moved away in disgust.

76

Stout an breezy, the loon of the laz would shuck himself up on the dancefloor and hunchback his body to the sweat of the set, the sacred, the bounding bass slugging at the stomp, shaling his making of the money to the honey, even as his knees crackled interference and his heart peddled at the metal of life.

It wasn't graceful and it wasn't good but the passionate brutality with which he moved across the floor was enough to stalk a claim on whatever territory he invaded. In the land of the blind, the one-eyed can is swing, flailing arms and stompbox feet that pounded concrete back to stand as sand, his dancing was a form of martial art, with all the balletic beauty of a street fight. And the more he moved, the less he drank and the less he drank, the longer he could stand and no one would need to slump him in the corner until throwing out time. Everyone has their moves and in general those moved would move they out of the Loon's a-way as he careened like a pinball between the clusters, often wailing his way out of the fringes where he could do less harm and back to the be-all and end-all. As courting couples would try to mirror themselves, the Loon would appear like a rockslide which only the deft of footwork could avoid. In the grit and the grain, he guessed they loved him for it, as in unholy drunk he blundered his soles and brokered their foals.

It was at one such event, and in the eventide of the evening, that some way or the other he clattered between Soya and Sister. A few years younger and let off the parental leash to visit her sibling in the city, Sister was new to this world of possible nightmares and while she'd maybe met the dandies of their world and Soya had steered her clear of the Nicodemian clutch, she'd never before encountered the steamroller that was the Loon Lazoon in full throttle flow. And just as a small hill looks impressive to one who has never seen their like before, so was Sister taken in by the man mountain dancing the dervish in front of her.

77

But Sister had been so impressed enough to lead the Loon to a seat of a sit, where the sweat of his knackers-yard-knees could recover some of their plausible dignity and they could talk above the world and it's nap. And talk he did and in his latter dreams still does, svengalic Laz rebuilding the world in his rambling image and Sister hanging on to every spellbound word of his chaos, replying in nods and smiles as much as his pauses for thought would allow, them holding shy hands as he reeled the roll into righting, turning the tale of the new, young rebels from the pedestrianist visions of Nicodemus and into the revolutionary rapture of Camilo Torres' torrential sermons. Even the blind could be dismissed into submission by the fireworks he laid before her, the half-drunk electro-glide orchestrations he painted across the universe and it's bindings.

In the innocence of her years, Sister had never come across anything so mesmeric, like opening the door to the wild conjure-man, mojo hand at hand and wailing the thrust of his gris-gris as he swept her into his lime.

Someone like Soya, of course, would've born the onslaught of his frantic before countering the weight of words with so many of her own, twisting Lazoon back on to his heels to flounder in her peels of laughter, but Sister was young, or maybe too joyous to want to bring the mystery of this magician to an end by looking behind the curtain to find the ruby slippers were only coloured glass.

Such was the brim of the bram and they never did dance the fandango no more and the castanets of his drinking hit a wall for the evening as they talked and talked, or he did at least in his broken memory until of a sudden hudden did the music die and the lights went on and on and two steps ahead and Soya came looking again so motherly protective for her little sis. Not that he couldn't be trusted with... well... with anything, but Fircle was taken the faken aback at just how quickly the big sis appeared to restore some chaperone sense to the universal.

"So will you be coming back up again?"

"In a few weeks," she replied, still a-smile and it may have been the first time he'd let her get a word in edgeways, "half-term is coming up soon."

"Oh, good, good," and he looked up to Soya for a gift of approval. Her face was implacably stolid. Damn, she was a fearsome and terrifying being!

"Come on you," she said as she took Sister by her spare right hand, but Sister still held on to his, looking into the bloodshot and bleared eyes of the Loon Lazoon with what he could only understand as love as he had no other frame of reference and no other grasp of life's bleaker emotions. And then they kissed a single, gentle kiss and she was gone.

78

Suki Danvers was a little redhead with a passion for history who would maybe in years to come lead him the length of the country looking at ruined buildings and maybe one day bear him a child or maybe more but at that moment she was just another spike-haired member of Fircle's audience as he held forth on the coming revolution, an open bottle of red wine in each hand that he swug from in alternating current. Before Sister could gather any thoughts of return, Fircle had fallen in drunken love, longing for a solace to raise him from his addictions but always unable to breach the walls of their natural indifference to his all-too-human existence. Following on, he found himself cast out of everyone's sight, beyond even the bolt of sibleyetic sexism, to wander as the last great auk did in its final quest for extinction. And while he tried to hold to the hills and sing of the setting sun, the word came calling from death's own hand that Pop was soon to pass.

Following Pop's death, Fircle moved back to help look after Ma, giving up his room with visions of never being able to return. Life began to disintegrate with Suki as the only thing he could see as a constant, beyond the need to destroy all memory and pain. In between the phone calls and her visits, he and Ma would drink through the vodka and the brandy, each also taking the big yellow pills to make it through til morning. As a consequence, the House of Heaven also began to dissipate, with people moving on and beyond.

It came again to Maus to save him once again from the private hell into which he'd sunk. While he walked with Cain in the wilderness, she made the calls, filled the forms and paid the ferryman to bring him back across the river, moving him into a two-bed flat with her in the Chancellery, a u-shaped block of flats slap-bang in the centre of Hateville but just a road crossing away from the Pyrotechnic. With her at the helm, Suki at the side and Nicodemus as a next-door neighbour, Fircle began to learn to live in the world of people again, leaving Ma to find her own way back from the underworld with just Sophocles as her guide. All that Fircle had been doing was drinking and crying while his brother had been carrying his own grief and theirs as well. So he ran to escape from his tears to return to a space where his longing for the golden brown tenderness of the fool could smother the ashes and dust that fell upon his grave thoughts and the ceaseless guilt of every action that he had ever undertaken.

79

Regret is a space of waste and time. The physics of expectant motherhood plays a plague on the drums of mismeaning and leaves you owing a debt to humanity. But still was Fircle regretting the netting he had hung his carcass in. Four hundred years too late he would still unwind the wound of pride and wonder the what ifs, the buts, the maybelline why can't you be trues? Age is an inappropriate measure of the meat and offal of circumstance. Time doesn't heal and absinthe doesn't make the harp glow fondue. It is no use trying to go back to find your mammaried memories as the loves you laboured are lost for good or eel. Sandwich it betwixt your drums and sonofagun yourself to the inclement walls. The arrow of time has flown in a broken wind and fallen at the feet of science. You canst go back, my son. You canst grow black the bleakered split and flit to mother's aghast at the screen. All those you knew no more to be dead to the dread. He drazzled in thought as time had gone, now dreadful lacerate it's goad blown out of inproportion. Last year was dead. Last decade. Last month. Yesterday, even, then lays in the lie of ruin a-wreck, the smart-meter of its landscape yet a wasteland ne'er to be trod nae more.

Pray forth for the giveness. Beg desper the need to be told all that has been done is drift in the whirlwinds. All the fuck of Fircle needed ever was an arm across his shoulder, a temple leant to his, a soothsayer's sound to salve the sins of the heart and then feast off the flesh. All ever was needed was the cotton-wool comfort, the safety from sorrow's embrace. Instead all he found whenever he awoke was the tremor and the fear, the knowledge of the ledge on the precipice's edge as all he could be giving. When you live in the abyss, the abyss also lives in your sieve. There is no escapade. There is no blister to renege your will against the floor of your fate, the beating breast-bone platitudes cut to the shreds across the killing floor, eating the mind from inside and burning out each socket til the tears will no longer justify the means of the end. There is no piafed regret. There is no hope but the grave thought of the grave.

80

Sometime or another's mother's other, he was picked up snapping his anchors in the middle of The Clampdown, deep in a mezcaled wormhole hidden, the dope of no hope, the fool and the fiend and the mystic drum all rolled into one with the poppied chaff, the sleeting of the beating raining down of the day. The screaming in his head never ceasing, never ending, never the shirk of respite's mist, the noises never quiet to a stop, just scream and scream again, the howl of every horror. All the old faces had gone to the wave of the grave, cut down by the gasp of winter and the cruciform liver, the swing of the ring and the cuffs and the crush of the final fist in the ethanol night. All was dead in the garden. All was but screaming in the lock. The hallucined eyes wide at the nut, the circumstance of hell's changes, the devil's chord, the fate of the gentry smoothing the realms of congressed time: compendium gone; market shattered by junk; the downstairs store he'd bought a Dizzy 10" vinyl gone to the ghost of old summers, n' more red braces, n' more the railway workers threads, n' more the kerb at Canal Bridge where he'd spent wasted hours wasted, wasted, and oh for the opiad infusion and oh for the grope of the bottle's kiss, it's clayed and cloying hand be-filtered through metal eyelids embletic of symptomatic rejection, turned outside of the inside, the pitied screams aylering out through the scam of the universe: No more the wishful wist of laudenum skies of rooftop romance to be brokered as broken on the despot wheels of wisdom, the cartwright wringing hands, the deal of Delia'd eyes lost to a languid dream forgot at the first of huddled hurdles; no more the flailing romeo'd rodeo to a juliet of the shorn Viola of the long lost pause an the final fated gasp; no more the chance perchance of Sister blistering at the inside mind, the lost cadavers of the lithe writhe of the turks, the chiving mcgurks of nickelodeons of time in the no more of midnight's laid at the hush of the lush, the catastrophe of the final far enigma'd pavilions twinned in sacrificial falling away to the tempt to, thrown beneath myriad wheels and wail the nay, the eclipse is gone at dawn, the Irish fighting-stick blown to the wind of the wind, a whim of candy, a shock of the green-skinned zealousy, in pantheons of parthenons heralding immajestic twists; n' more the birth rebirth the death re-death, choked in smoke, letting him follow you down as crashed symphonic harmonics of organ grind to the rusted bone converted to ink jerusalems, angered at the doghouse of bitter standards betraying the baying wives of cop-sheet calamity, honduran by complex staves of pin whistle gloried; no more the jankled wail; n' more the holied plaintiff speaking in deadbeat tongues, in ginsbergian shoes shedded and sandal soaked; no more the childish billy-o bought in the stacks, the racks, the ravens plundering blind señoritas stoned in the rainy days of cypriot avenues, breathing in and out as sleep slipped into the mid-stream; no more the hilliard of eyes retained, Corined in the corral of a goat's last grimace before the formulaic fall; no more the gas works walk in chains; no more the klook-a-mopped refrain in wild heart, attacks of flail, the platted platitudes of stricken cosmonauts turn pail, turn their carpenter's grail and throw the innocent victims down in jail, carp the feet of blaired peach-murderers, their cosh in hand, their cock and glands, the badly bandaged scalp davis'd in the triumphant stance of orphic prisms of underworld, the underwear world, the undisc-wold folds and falls; no more the cheeky grin, the bitter taste of gin in the Hotspur's face; no more the ruin, no more the race; no more the lynyrd limerick haunting in rizla'd papier maché mounts of now unreliable desires, of unfathomable fires of Joan's forgotten pyre in the mystery train of the presleyed night; no more love quest, the journeyed gate, the fate of the fallen dead turned turquoise by inviolate pride all praised and formic funking; no open doors no more, no chances of the chase, the lover's escape, the torn tears drained from empty sockets, lockets of hair, rockets of bald-scratch turkey damned in wrapping, the foiled factions of no more the ingrid bergman smile, the skip, the cause lost and loving of the moment, just the wailing wailing wailing betwixt the between of the unknown scene as officers harried their shot gun-dreams at the windmilled harangue the falling down splinters of bloodshot inserenity, the clucking and the boiled bottle stark with the concrete clatter, the aerating tears snowflake their tantrumed decay into stolen air with the bellowed horseshit moan pinned to the dust of red-checked, misfired misery; no more the lacrimaed christ the bastard lovelorn, the knee in the back and Maria black as sirened escorts but just the cave and the doctored cocktail of downered drowned and tranquil inject to tame the turbulent and strap-the-bugger-down to the cot and traffic him throughout the scything sun of the laudenum afternoon for assessment. One hundred and thirty six stones to be stepped in a three-day excursion whacked up for the first forty-eight on the heady party selection of hundreds and thousands deposited and supposited in contradictory motion, the prostrate prostate slabbed in white TB'd sheets of the smallest pox, the peeling ceiling of old municipality and the joys of jif in the walls and bleach in the corners, the howl of strangers strangled through their pending unrepentant darkness of noon with mopping men stood in the cold fluorescence of the open doorway discussing the merits of fresh pickings and young plunder in the wicked hours of slept nurses and catatonia in the suite of the substance abused to keep the cats from yowling as to the mow the meadow at speed to the seventy two gates of the hope of hate and the hate of hope despaired into the broth of loss, the despots of discarded rendition trammelled down through the skin of the skull so that all it can do from the end of the rays of the day is cry and cry and burn out the balls with the dead-sea-salt of your tears.

Editor's Note:

Alfie's books take a lot of time to edit. We make a lot of
suggested changes and most he sends back rejected.
Some do get through – mostly odd bits of punctuation
and the occasional spell-checker cock up. Then, just as
you think you're nearing the end, a comma will
disappear to be replaced by a whole new section.
Generally, if a word looks wrong, appears to be mis-
spelt or isn't even a word in anyone's language, he'll tell
you that's what it's meant to be, that it's there for a
reason. So good luck with that.

- F.H.

Also by Alfie Cooke

Music
Beginning Free Improvisation
Music from Within a Rogue Nation (Bb, C, Eb)
Songbook Vol. 1 (Eb edition)
Symphony No. 1 (Blues Adagio) full score

Art
Fragments of a Memory: The Art of Annie Poulter

Fiction
Learning Goat
Babylon Arcades

Poetry
The Grown Man Fell To His Knees And Wept Just Like A
    Baby (as Alfie Howard)
Unknown Languages

Religion
The Ethics of Revolutionary Buddhism

Printed in Great Britain
by Amazon

20627570R00120